GAME, SET, Matched

IVY BAILEY
GAME, SET, Matched

SIMON & SCHUSTER
London New York Amsterdam/Antwerp Sydney/Melbourne Toronto New Delhi

First published in Great Britain in 2025 by Gallery Kids,
an imprint of Simon & Schuster UK Ltd

Written by Katy Birchall © Simon & Schuster
Cover illustrations © 2025 Jacqueline Lu

This book is copyright under the Berne Convention.
No reproduction without permission. All rights reserved.

1 3 5 7 9 10 8 6 4 2

Simon & Schuster UK Ltd, 1st Floor
222 Gray's Inn Road, London WC1X 8HB

For more than 100 years, Simon & Schuster has championed authors and the stories they create. By respecting the copyright of an author's intellectual property, you enable Simon & Schuster and the author to continue publishing exceptional books for years to come. We thank you for supporting the author's copyright by purchasing an authorized edition of this book. No amount of this book may be reproduced or stored in any format, nor may it be uploaded to any website, database, language-learning model, or other repository, retrieval, or artificial intelligence system without express permission. All rights reserved. Inquiries may be directed to Simon & Schuster, 222 Gray's Inn Road, London WC1X 8HB or RightsMailbox@simonandschuster.co.uk

www.simonandschuster.co.uk
www.simonandschuster.com.au
www.simonandschuster.co.in

Simon & Schuster Australia, Sydney
Simon & Schuster India, New Delhi

The authorised representative in the EEA is Simon & Schuster Netherlands BV, Herculesplein 96, 3584 AA Utrecht, Netherlands. info@simonandschuster.nl

A CIP catalogue record for this book is available from the British Library.

ISBN 978-1-3985-4688-2
eBook ISBN 978-1-3985-4715-5
eAudio ISBN 978-1-3985-4714-8

This book is a work of fiction. Names, characters, places and incidents are either the product of the author's imagination or are used fictitiously. Any resemblance to actual people living or dead, events or locales is entirely coincidental.

Printed and Bound in the UK using 100% Renewable Electricity at CPI Group (UK) Ltd

*For the Wimbledon Juniors,
our tennis stars of the future*

CHAPTER ONE

The ball drops down towards me from the sky.

I move my right foot back, rotating my body sideways, and stretch out my left arm as high as possible. My right hand brings my tennis racket swinging up and over my head, smashing the ball with full force. It soars over the net, landing with a loud smack on the opposite service line, and our opponents helplessly watch it bounce high out of reach.

'*Yes!*' I cry, balling my hand into a fist in celebration.

'Game, set and match,' my coach, Nick, calls out from the side of the court.

I spin round to face Tom, who is strolling towards me from the baseline. He tucks his racket under his arm, and we high-five before moving to meet our opponents at the net.

'Nice smash to finish on. I wish I had your power, Billie,' Scarlett says with a grin, shaking my hand and then Tom's before balancing her tennis racket on the ground between her feet so she can redo her ponytail.

Her doubles partner, Caleb, sighs, reaching over the net to rub my shoulder after he's shaken our hands. 'You played *amazingly*,' he drawls in his posh accent, his thumb tracing over the ridge of my sports bra strap beneath my tank top as he gives my shoulder a squeeze.

Tom notices and raises his eyebrows at me, amused.

'Thanks – you did, too,' I reply politely as he drops his hand on Nick's approach.

'Excellent, all of you,' Nick declares. 'A great match.'

'Hardly a close one,' Scarlett remarks, wiping the sheen of sweat from her forehead. 'I feel like I'm about to collapse, the way these two had us running around the court.' She picks up her tennis racket and points it at Tom. 'No one's a match for the Dawson twins.'

'They're hard to beat,' Nick agrees, 'but you put up a great fight. Scarlett, beautiful spin on your forehand; Caleb, some great moments from you today – you just have to try to control your temper, yeah?'

'I actually *dropped* my racket after that double fault,' Caleb claims, his cheeks growing pinker. 'I didn't throw it. I can understand why it looked that way, though.'

'Okay,' Nick says, clearly unconvinced. 'Right, go get some water, people.'

While the other three wander over to their tennis bags at the side of the court, I linger with Nick at the net a moment longer.

'Any pointers for me, Coach?'

He sighs, folding his arms. 'You know what I'm going to say, Billie. Nice focus, lots of power, but not enough risk. You were predictable.'

'What? We won in straight sets!'

'In a friendly doubles match at your county club,' Nick says pointedly, his eyebrows raised. 'I'm not saying that *these* opponents could read you, but the ones you'll face in a few weeks might. If you and Tom really want to win a junior title at Wimbledon this year – and as your coach, you know I want that too – then you're going to have to stop playing it so safe. Relax into the game a bit more; have some fun with it.'

My jaw tenses and I look down at the ground.

There's a picture on the mantelpiece of me and Tom holding tennis rackets as toddlers on a grass court, one racket placed in Tom's little hands as he stares at the photographer in confusion, while I'm busy chewing the frame of another. It's a great photo, and Dad loves to point at it and say to guests: 'You see? They practically grew up on the court.'

And it's true, we did, thanks to him. After school, he would take the two of us to our local club in Berkshire and we'd dutifully stand on one side of the net while he gently hit the ball to each of us by turn, cheering so enthusiastically at our returns that we would burst into giggles. As we got older, we took joint lessons at weekends, and spent long hours after school practising drills and playing games, each hoping that we would get to be the one to go home and tell Dad we'd won against the other. Tom mostly got that honour. He seemed so naturally talented, it felt unfair. I would come home, flustered, sweating, stroppy from losing, while he returned unfazed and looking as though he hadn't broken a sweat.

I owe it to Tom for giving me the competitive streak you need to win. If it wasn't for my burning desire to beat my unfairly gifted seven-minutes-younger brother, I wouldn't have been out on the courts whenever I had a spare moment practising my serves, focusing on my footwork, hitting groundstrokes over and over and over again. I think it's probably a good thing that Tom isn't a competitive or confrontational person, because then we might not have become as close as we are. Where I'm determined and focused, he's gentle and composed.

Tom's talent was spotted early, and the club suggested our dad speak to Nick Webb, a former pro who worked there, about training him. I remember Nick coming to watch Tom play with me so he could study his form before he agreed to coach him. As I tied my shoelaces before walking onto the court, I decided that I would play better than ever before. Dad got cross at me for hitting winners when I was meant to be setting up points for Tom and drawing out the rallies so that Nick could see Tom's range.

'Don't be so aggressive, Billie,' he snapped when I concluded a rally with a powerful volley. He came closer to speak to me through gritted teeth so Nick couldn't hear: 'You're showing off. Don't ruin this for your brother.'

He was right; I was showing off. But I didn't ruin things for Tom. When our practice came to an end, Nick happily agreed to train him, but he also extended the offer to include me.

Under Nick's guidance, both of us did well in our singles events, but it was in the doubles events that we really shone. In our early teens, we hoped that we might be good enough to make it – Dad definitely thought that Tom was – but we eventually had to accept that while we may be great at tennis, neither of us would be one of *the* greats.

We just weren't good enough.

Tom handled that much better than I did. Tennis was my life – I'd sacrificed so much for my passion. School grades, other hobbies, friends' parties, boyfriends. All these normal experiences had been missed in the hope that I'd go pro. The two of us have still played on the national circuit and we've made our mark in doubles events – but we've turned eighteen. Having just completed our A-Levels, this summer draws our junior tennis career to a close.

Then came the announcement: Wimbledon to host a junior mixed doubles event for the first time ever. It will be the *perfect* farewell to the circuit before we go to university.

Our rankings mean we qualify, and while other junior players will likely focus more on their singles performance with the doubles tournament as back-up, Tom and I can put all our time and energy into playing as a pair, aligning our strengths, working together as a slick and intimidating team. He has the precision; I have the power. And I've always been strongest on grass. Our doubles performance on the circuit has already set tongues wagging.

The junior brother and sister team no one saw coming, claimed a headline in one of the recent International Tennis Federation articles. I printed it out and stuck it on my wall. Tom rolled his eyes when he saw it hanging above my bed.

'It's a backhanded compliment, Billie,' he said, shaking his head. 'I'd have thought you'd be angry that we've flown under the radar the past few years. Why would you want to look at that every day and be reminded that no one noticed us?'

But I'm used to being underestimated. And I know how it feels to prove someone wrong. Nothing makes you feel more powerful. Looking at that article every day motivates me to give my all to this game until Wimbledon ends this summer.

This unforeseen brother-and-sister team is bowing out with a bang.

'You know how much I want to win this,' I tell Nick now, bringing my eyes back up to meet his. 'I don't understand what you mean when you say I'm playing it too safe.'

'Yes, you do,' he counters. 'Your entire focus is on not making mistakes when, sometimes, you need to go for the win.'

'What do you call that last smash?' I point out defensively.

'A predictable shot.' He shrugs. 'Up against the right opponents, they would have seen it coming and it might have been returned. It was difficult, but not impossible.'

He watches as I frown, sighing in exasperation.

'Billie,' Nick continues gently, 'it's my job to pick out the tiniest details. At Wimbledon, you'll be playing against the tennis stars of the future. The best of the best. I'm not saying you're not brilliant – you and Tom are outstanding players, especially together. I think there's a very real chance you could go far in this tournament.'

I glance at him hopefully. 'Yeah?'

'Yes,' he confirms. 'That's why you need to be prepared for me to question absolutely everything about Tom's and your performance over the next few weeks. You need to work on mixing things up a little. Tom needs to work on his fitness.'

That takes me by surprise. 'He does?'

'He looked a little slower out there today,' Nick remarks, his brow furrowed as he peers over my shoulder at Tom, who's scrolling through his phone as he waits at the side of the court. 'It's like he has less energy. Maybe he's not sleeping well.'

'I'll speak to him,' I promise.

I notice Nick's eyes drift to someone else who has arrived on the court and I follow his eyeline. Harley Pierce: Nick's nephew and, by an unfortunate stroke of luck, my next-door neighbour. Unsurprisingly, despite the fact he's been on the courts for all of one minute, he's already sauntered up to Scarlett with that cocky smile of his and, leaning one arm on the net post, is wasting no time in attempting to charm her. I have to fight the urge to roll my eyes, hoping that Scarlett will be smart enough to see that Harley Pierce is a walking red flag.

He runs a hand through his dark messy hair as he smiles. What's absolutely infuriating is how high his ITF ranking is when he puts as little effort as possible into his tennis. He's only a member of this club thanks to his uncle, and if it weren't for the number of girls who play here, I doubt Harley would ever set foot on these courts. I have no time for someone like him.

'Thanks for the pointers, Coach,' I say, turning my attention back to Nick. 'I'll work on it. You don't have to worry.'

'I never do with you, Billie Dawson,' Nick says with a laugh. 'The hardest-working kid I know.'

I see Scarlett heading towards the locker rooms with Caleb as I turn to go and flick my glance to Harley, still leaning on the net post. Either Harley's chat didn't make the cut or he works incredibly fast. Knowing Scarlett, it's the former.

'You looked good out there today, Dawson,' Harley remarks, his dark eyes settling on mine. 'I've said it before – if ever you're looking for someone to play with, you know where to find me. I enjoy a challenge.' A playful smile creeps across his lips before he adds, 'And I reckon we'd be a great match.'

I look him up and down, and snort dismissively as I walk towards the exit.

'In your dreams, Harley,' I mutter.

CHAPTER TWO

'How did practice go today?' Dad asks Tom, pulling out his chair at the top of the table and sitting down. He notices me offering him the salad bowl and takes it. 'Oh, thank you, Billie.'

'It was good,' Tom answers absent-mindedly, lowering his pet tortoise, Rufus, down onto the table.

Dad chuckles. 'Is that all I get? "It was good"? A little more detail would be helpful, please.' He notices Rufus and gives Tom a *don't even think about it* look. 'No tortoises at the table, Tom. Please return him upstairs while we eat.'

'He's not in anyone's way,' Tom protests affectionately, admiring Rufus.

'Thomas,' Dad says in a warning tone.

Tom sighs. 'Fine,' he huffs, picking up Rufus before grabbing a lettuce leaf from the bowl in Dad's hand and drifting out of the room.

Tom's obsessed with animals, and Rufus is the latest in a

long string of pets he's had over the years – hamsters, guinea pigs, fish – he's marvelled over all them and his head is full of fascinating animal facts. Rufus lives in his room along with his pet gecko, Claude.

'As soon as I move out and go to university, I'm getting a dog,' Tom grumbled to me the other day when Dad said no to his request once again.

'Yeah, because I'm sure the student halls will have no problem with that.'

He responded to my heavy sarcasm with an irritated look. 'I'll find somewhere else to live. I don't care.'

'Law degrees are intense,' I reminded him wearily. 'You won't have time for a dog.'

He'd fallen silent at that, his expression growing hard and pensive. He knew I was right.

Having helped himself to salad, Dad carefully places the bowl down into an empty space on the table. He reaches for his napkin, unfolding it and placing it over his knees to protect his suit trousers, before loosening his tie and undoing the top button of his shirt. As a lawyer himself, Dad works long hours and is rarely home in time for dinner on weekdays, but if ever he is, he'll be in a suit, having just rushed through the door from the office. Mondays to Fridays, Dad is always in a suit, even when he works from home, and at weekends, he still dresses smartly – suit trousers or chinos with a shirt, but no tie.

The only time he ever wears shorts is on a tennis court.

Sitting next to him now, I clash with his formal attire in the oversized black hoodie and faded coral shorts that I threw on after showering. Dad and I don't really look very much alike – we have the same hazel eyes, but that's where the similarities end. Tom got Dad's strong jaw and curly brown hair, while I've always been likened to Mum: the same long, wavy honey-blonde hair and smattering of freckles across my nose and cheeks.

Dad waits until Tom has returned to repeat his request: 'So, come on then – a little more detail about your practice today?'

'Ask Billie,' Tom says, glumly stabbing at some broccoli.

It's obvious when I've been in charge of dinner, like tonight – seasoned lean meat and a variety of vegetables are usually on the menu, something high energy and balanced, as well as delicious. When Tom cooks, we get plain pasta with grated cheese sprinkled on top.

Giving him an unimpressed look, Dad rests his elbows on the table and, on Tom's advice, turns his attention to me. 'Any embellishment on what your brother's told me?'

'We started with a gentle warm-up, went into drills –' I pause to shoot Tom a sly smile – 'during which Tom struggled to return my serves ...'

'I told you earlier, I'm not feeling great. I have a sore throat. And I only missed, like, two,' he grumbles.

'You missed five.'

He narrows his eyes at me. 'Of *course* you counted them.'

'Got to keep you on your toes,' I say innocently. 'What else are older sisters for?'

'Older by only seven minutes.'

'Even the day we were born, I beat you.'

'Shut up.'

'You shut up.'

'*You* shut up.'

'Both of you, *please*,' Dad interjects with a heavy sigh. He gives me a stern look. 'Continue. Warm-up, then drills, and then ...'

He trails off, gesturing for me to take over.

'Then we finished the training with a friendly match against another doubles pair at the club, Scarlett and Caleb.'

'Hmm.' Dad furrows his brow. 'Do I know Caleb?'

'He's the one with the mop of blond hair,' Tom informs him, before he exacts his revenge on me with a wicked grin. 'The one who dated Billie.'

'We did *not* date,' I hiss, kicking him under the table.

'They did date,' Tom tells Dad smugly. 'But she dumped him—'

'Shut *up*, Tom.'

'And ever since, he follows her around like a lovesick puppy.'

'Oh my god, you are so annoying!'

'I do *love* you so, Billie,' Tom says in an overly posh accent, flicking his hair back dramatically. 'Come, let us go galloping on horses into the sunset!'

'Ugh, he does not sound like that,' I argue, trying my best to suppress a smile, but I can't help it. He may be quiet and shy around everyone else, but Tom never fails to make me laugh. 'Why are you the *most* annoying person on the planet?'

'It's my duty! What else are younger brothers for?'

'Only seven minutes younger,' I mutter.

Dad clears his throat pointedly and both of us fall silent, turning to look at him.

'Do you think it might be possible,' he begins, reaching for his glass of red wine, 'for me to get one ounce of sense from at least *one* of my eighteen-year-old *grown-up* children? Or am I going to have to resort to phoning Nick and disturbing his Friday evening to hear about your day?'

Sitting up straight, I take a deep breath. 'In short, we won.'

'Course you did,' Dad says, breaking into a smile as he lowers his glass. 'No one is a match for Tom's forehand.'

The effect of his comment is instant.

Tensing, my eyes drop to my plate as I move my food around it aimlessly. Tom shifts in his seat. I glance up at Dad, who continues eating, oblivious to any change in the atmosphere.

'My forehand wasn't what got us the win today,' Tom says. 'It was Billie who won us the match. She was taking no prisoners.'

'Oh?' Dad looks at me in surprise. 'Well done, Billie.'

'Thanks, Dad,' I say quietly, before shooting Tom a small but grateful smile.

'I *knew* that playing with Tom would be a good thing for your game,' Dad says, jabbing his loaded fork at me. 'When you play with the best, you learn from the best.'

My smile falters. Tom winces. Dad chews his mouthful.

'Dad, no, that's not …' Tom sighs, looking physically pained at the awkwardness of the conversation, appealing to me with his large hazel eyes, the exact same colour as mine and Dad's. 'Billie doesn't need my help; she's—'

'Oh, that reminds me,' Dad cuts in over him, dabbing at his mouth with his napkin, 'one of my colleagues asked if you would consider giving a talk at his daughter's school.'

Tom looks horrified. Public speaking is his worst nightmare.

'*What?*' He glances at me, but I feel as bewildered as him. 'Why would anyone want me to give a school talk?'

Dad barks with laughter. 'Why? Because you're a former Wimbledon champion.'

I feel a sharp stab in my chest. I know how this conversation plays out. I've experienced it many times. It never gets any less painful.

'Dad …' Tom says, closing his eyes.

'I know it was a few years ago,' Dad says with a wave of his hand, 'but it doesn't matter. Thomas Dawson, winner of the

Fourteen and Under Boys' Singles event at the Wimbledon Championships.'

I swallow the lump building in my throat. The year Tom won at Wimbledon was the same year I made the final of the 14&Under Girls' Singles event.

It doesn't matter how long ago it was; I can still remember the moment my competitor hit her winning shot. I can hear the thud of the ball as it hit the grass and soared out of my reach. I can hear the roar of her supporters. I remember exactly how I felt: ashamed and embarrassed, the disappointment weighing down on me so hard, I could barely walk over to shake her hand at the net.

And every time someone talks about Tom's big win, I feel it all over again.

'I was a kid; it's not even a proper contest,' Tom says hurriedly, while I sip my water, pretending Dad's overt pride doesn't make me want to cry.

'Britain's leading star in junior tennis at that point,' Dad continues, exactly on cue. 'And still a shining light in the sport today, despite the fact you've decided not to go pro.'

'It wasn't a choice, Dad. I was never—'

'If you'd put your mind to it, Tom, you could have,' Dad tells him sternly. 'You're such a beautiful player; you've always stood out. Anyway, it wasn't to be, and that's fine. You're going to make a top lawyer, much better than me, I'm sure of that.'

Dad chuckles. Tom doesn't say anything.

'So, yes, my colleague's daughter is ten or so, I think,' Dad continues cheerfully. 'He thought that you would be an excellent person to speak in an assembly and inspire the children to put down their phones and play some sport! I thought—'

Dad's phone rings and he quickly pulls it out of his pocket to check the screen.

'Hang on.' The legs of his chair scrape against the floor as he pushes it back to stand up. 'Sorry, I have to take this,' he tells us, before answering the phone and hurrying out of the kitchen to his office.

We hear the door shut behind him, his voice becoming muffled.

Tom exhales, looking up at me. 'Bills, are you—'

'I'm fine.'

'But—'

'Tom, I'm *fine*,' I insist through a fixed smile. 'It's nice he's so proud of you.'

He slumps back in his chair, his eyes lifting to the ceiling. 'I honestly wish I'd never won.'

'Don't say that,' I say, giving his leg a nudge under the table as I feel a pang of guilt. 'You deserved it.' I hesitate, before adding loftily, 'It makes it even more impressive that today I beat Britain's *former leading star in junior tennis*.'

His expression softens. 'You did not beat me. I missed a couple of your serves.'

'Five,' I correct.

Chuckling, he shakes his head and we share a conspiratorial smile before both of us get back to our meal. Keen to shift the conversation, I ask him a meaningless question about a movie he mentioned yesterday and he launches into his dorky analysis of it.

I may be smiling and nodding along, but I'm still recovering from the conversation with Dad. If I close my eyes, I can still see Mum in the stand that day at Wimbledon, cheering me on. I remember her clapping enthusiastically, as if there were some hope I might pull it back. By then, we knew that her illness was going to get worse and there wasn't anything anyone could do. She was thin and frail, wrapped in layers at the side of the court despite the warm day, but it didn't stop her being the loudest among the spectators. The outing drained her. She became too weak to attend matches after that.

We lost her a couple of months later.

'This year serves to remind us that through times of darkness, there are always glimmers of light and hope,' Dad said at her funeral, his glistening eyes landing on Tom and me as we sat front row, hand in hand, each of us desperately trying to be strong for the other.

I knew Dad was talking about Tom's win. Tom had brought a glimmer of light.

But not me.

My loss became my deepest shame, and I have never been

able to forgive myself. I overdid it that day; I tried to go for big points and I made too many forced errors. I panicked and lost control of my mind, which meant I lost control of the court. I let everyone down. I let myself down. And I let my mum down at the worst possible time. She *needed* glimmers of light, then.

That's why I'm so determined to win this summer. That's why I've been on the court practising whenever possible; working on my fitness every spare moment I've got; eating the right things; studying doubles tactic videos in the evenings; turning down parties that all my friends are going to now that A-Levels are done and the holidays have started.

I mean it when I say that Wimbledon introducing a junior mixed doubles tournament this year, the final year Tom and I can qualify, is fate. Sometimes I think it's a message from her. Another chance to make my family proud. My last chance to make up for what happened, to honour her memory with a Wimbledon win.

And I won't let anything or anyone get in my way.

CHAPTER THREE

Melrose's finest 💋🖤

> **Jess**
> Happy Saturday, bitches!
> What's the plan for tonight?

> **Kat**
> I heard that Rambler's is going to be good
> Usually a few school lot there from Melrose

> **Jess**
> Perfect! Meet you there at 7?
> I said I'd have dinner at home

> **Kat**
> Sounds good to me!
> Hopefully by 7 I'll feel more alive

Kat
Last night killed me
Tell me why I thought Jägerbombs were a good idea?
And tell me why you didn't stop me?

Jess
I tried
You told me to fuck off

Kat
Sounds reasonable

Jess
It was a great night
We missed you, Billie!

Kat
We really did
You're coming tonight, right?

Jess
Yeah, course she is!
You deserve a night off, Bills

Kat
Wimbledon is in the bag!
Come ouuutttttt

Jess
It's good for you to have a break
Good for the brain

Kat
Good for the soul

Jess
And good for our souls to have you there
The conversation is shit without you

Kat
It's true
That's why I ordered the Jägerbombs
To make Jess's book chat seem interesting

Jess
Hey!
You said we should make our own book club!?!?!?

Kat
That was the Jäger talking
Sweet, naive Jess

Jess
See, Billie?
We need you
You're the only person who loves books as much as I do

Billie
Hey! Sorry, I've just seen all these

Jess
Let me guess
You were on the court

Kat
We're meeting you at Rambler's at 7
It's a 10 min walk from your house
So if you don't show, we'll come get you

Billie
Huh
Sounds like I don't have a choice

Jess
WHOA! Chill out, Billie!
So much enthusiasm for a night out with your best friends!

Kat
Yeah, don't overdo it!
Play it cool for once!

Billie
You two are idiots

Kat
We love you too!!
See you at 7
Don't wear tennis gear

Billie
You think I'd show up
to a bar in tennis stuff?

Kat
Yes

> **Jess**
> Yes

> **Billie**
> Fair
> See you at 7 xx

I try not to feel guilty as I wait at the bar for one of the staff to notice me so I can put in an order, but it creeps up on me – a niggling voice at the back of my head telling me that if I drink and stay out too late, I'll be groggy in the morning and my game will be off. Tapping my fingers impatiently on the counter, I promise myself I'll get up early as always and go for a run, no matter how late I get home tonight.

'Jesus, Bills.' Jess sighs, leaning next to me and giving me a look. 'I can read you like a fucking book.'

I glance at her in confusion. 'What?'

'Could you relax, please? You're allowed one night off.'

'And in case you've forgotten, we've finished our A-Levels and *just left school*,' Kat interjects, checking the plunge neckline of her fitted black dress and flicking her softly curled hair back over her shoulder. 'Goodbye, Melrose! We're free now and meant to be having *fun*.'

I smile at them, heaving a sigh. 'You're right. Sorry. I'm going to stop worrying now.'

'Good. I need your full focus if you're going to be a

successful wing-woman,' Kat tells me in a low voice, surveying the crowded bar. 'There are so many hot guys in here tonight. And –' she gives Jess a pointed look – 'a lot of hot girls, too.'

'I've noticed,' Jess says, glancing around the crowd. 'They didn't go to Melrose, right? I hardly recognize anyone here.'

'*Yum*. Fresh blood,' Kat says, her eyes filled with excitement.

I laugh, before I turn my attention back to the bar. Kat may say she wants a wing-woman, but she definitely doesn't need one. She's so gorgeous, she's the centre of attention wherever she goes. She looks great tonight, too, her curly brown hair falling around her shoulders, her dark eyes framed by a perfectly executed bold-lined cat flick and heavy eyelashes, and a dress that clings to her envy-inducing curves. I already know she's going to be breaking hearts all over the continent as she moves from city to city on her dream trip around Europe, which she's been planning for as long as I can remember. Smart, funny, bold – it's hard not to fall in love with Kat.

Jess hasn't gone unnoticed, either, even if she'd rather that she did. She's the tallest of the three of us, and with her striking platinum-dyed hair, sharp cheekbones and full lips, she was scouted once by a model agency, but refused to even take their card. She's so averse to attention that she doesn't even have any social media. She loves a good night out, but her ideal evening would be at home alone, curled up with a book.

I maybe should have made a little more effort tonight – now

that I'm here, I feel underdressed in my baggy jeans, T-shirt and jacket, but I was so tired after training this afternoon, I didn't have the energy to pick out anything more glamorous. At least I brushed my hair, leaving it down in its natural waves over my shoulders, and I attempted a bit of make-up: a lick of mascara, sweep of bronzer and a nude-pink lip.

A voice near us cuts through the din: 'Your name is Kat, right?'

Jess and I both glance at the guy who has approached her. He has short fair hair and brown eyes, and he's *stacked*. I can already see from Kat's coy smile that she likes what she sees – she's always been a sucker for a guy who loves the gym. I recognize him, but I can't think from where. There's something familiar about him.

'That's right,' Kat replies, tilting her head.

'Then looks like we're destined to be together.'

She grins at his startling confidence. 'What makes you think that?'

'Because ... my name is Kit,' he tells her, his tongue flicking out to lick his lips. 'Kit and Kat, right? Kit Kat.'

Jess and I share an unimpressed look. But Kat throws her head back and laughs. A proper laugh, too, not a fake one. She's not being polite or trying to flirt. She actually enjoyed the joke. He looks thrilled at her reaction.

'Kit and Kat,' she repeats, gazing up at him from under her full eyelashes. 'Interesting. Maybe we were meant to meet.'

'I have to come clean, though. People don't call me Kit, even though it is my name,' he assures her, lifting his hands up. 'My friends call me Bards.'

'And why do they do that?' Kat replies.

'My surname is Bardsley. I've been Bards since forever.'

'Well then, nice to meet you, Bards.'

'Can I get you a drink?'

'Sure,' she says as he moves up to the bar on her other side.

She winks at me and then turns her back on us to face him properly.

'We may have lost Kat for the night,' Jess says to me in a low voice, chuckling. Her eyes light up as she spots a group leaving one of the tables nearby. 'I'm going to go grab that table before someone else does.'

'I'll bring the drinks over,' I say before she hurries off.

My full attention now back on the bar, I manage to finally get our order in, reaching for my phone to get ready to pay.

'That it?' the guy behind the bar asks as he reaches for a couple of glasses to start pouring the gin and tonics.

Before I can answer, someone slides into the space next to me to cut in: 'And one more of whatever she's having.'

Turning to look at the imposter, I roll my eyes when I realize who it is.

'Hello, Dawson.' Harley Pierce grins, shifting to face me, one elbow leaning on the bar. 'Nice to see you out in the wild for a change.'

'Whereas I'm sure the bar staff know you well here,' I say drily.

'I know you mean that as an insult,' he says, greatly amused, 'but I refuse to take it as one. We're young and free.' He gestures around the buzzing bar. 'Got to live while you can.'

'Thanks for the pearl of wisdom,' I mutter, craning my neck to watch the barman prepare our drinks, hoping he'll hurry up so I can exit this conversation swiftly.

'I think my friend likes your friend,' Harley comments, nodding to Kat.

'Ah, that's why he looks familiar!' I say, glancing over at Bards as it dawns on me. 'He's *your* mate. He likes to pick you up late at night and beep the horn really loudly with his music blaring for the whole street to enjoy!'

'That's him. He went to Burton Grammar with me.'

'I think I once had to ask him to pick up what was left of his spliff when he flicked it onto the street. He told me where to go – a real stand-up guy,' I say sarcastically.

'Maybe you caught him on a bad day.' Harley raises his eyebrows as Kat giggles at something Bards has just said. 'Looks like *she's* impressed by him.'

'Strange. Although, she *is* a few drinks down.'

He snorts. 'Ouch. I take it Bards hasn't won you over tonight then.'

'Aside from being aware of his terrible music taste and his fondness for weed and littering, I haven't had the pleasure of talking to him,' I say, getting my card up on my phone. 'But his "Kit Kat" line was a real hit. Brought the house down.'

'You know, Dawson,' he says, tilting his head at me, 'a lot of guys might be intimidated by your killer combination of sharp remarks and dry sarcasm – I, however, find it extremely attractive. Your glacial exterior does nothing to put me off.'

'Lucky me.'

'There, you see?' He places a palm on his chest. 'Sarcasm to die for.'

I shoot him a withering look.

'Don't you think we should hang out more?' he says, as though it's a brilliant idea that's just dawned on him. 'We live next door to each other and we have a lot in common.'

'I have more in common with Rufus than you.'

He looks confused. 'Who's Rufus?'

'My brother's tortoise.'

'Your brother has a *tortoise*? Huh.' He nods slowly, apparently impressed. 'Kind of cool.'

Lining the drinks up for me along the counter, the barman punches the amount I owe into the card machine and holds it out.

'No, wait, let me,' Harley says, getting his phone out. 'I want to get this.'

'It's fine,' I say, paying for the round and sliding him the drink he added in.

He raises his eyebrows. 'Thanks, Dawson. This works out very nicely for me.'

'Because your boldness to jump in on my order landed you a free drink?'

'Because now I owe *you* a drink,' he corrects, the corners of his lips twitching upwards. 'You'll have to let me take you for one.'

'Consider yourself debt-free. I insist.'

'Like a dagger to the heart.' He sighs. 'Come on, Dawson – it would be fun. You ever allow yourself some of that?'

'Some of what?' I ask, sliding my phone into my back pocket.

'Some *fun*.' His eyes flash at me mischievously. 'I meant what I said before – we've got a lot in common. We're both extraordinary tennis players. I'm not sure who is better, but we're probably on a similar level—'

'I could beat you with my eyes closed,' I say, deadpan.

'Our friends get on very well—'

'They literally just met.'

'*And* –' he glances around the room before lowering his voice to a conspiratorial whisper – 'we happen to be the two best-looking people in the room.'

'Wow. Does that line usually work?' I whisper back.

'It's never failed.'

'Well, then,' I begin, picking up my drinks, 'I guess there's a first time for everything.'

Shooting him a mock-sympathetic smile, I turn around and begin weaving my way through the crowd, hearing him chuckling alone where I left him.

CHAPTER FOUR

Bards is trying to convince us to go to an after-party.

I'm ready to go home, already dreading that early morning alarm, but I can tell that Kat and Jess are tempted.

'There's *loads* of people coming,' he insists, as I put my hands in my jacket pockets. 'It's at my mate's place. We can pick up booze on the way – there might be other stuff flying around too, if that's your style. Whatever you want, I can get it.'

Kat grins dopily as he winds an arm around her waist and pulls her into him. Jess and I share a look, while Harley is busy messaging on his phone.

'Thanks, but I'm happy with some beers. A party sounds fun,' Kat says, before turning to us. 'You two coming?'

Jess sighs. 'I don't know. Where is it?'

'It's about a five-minute walk from here. And there will be a lot of single girls,' Bards says, winking at her. 'I can make some introductions, get you in there.'

'Thanks for the offer, but I can introduce myself,' Jess replies, amused at the suggestion .

Bards exhales, squeezing Kat tighter. 'Not easy to win over, are they, your mates.'

'They have very high standards,' she agrees, beaming proudly at Jess. 'What are you thinking, Jess? You game? You know I won't go if you won't.'

'Ah come *on*, Jess,' Bards pleads, his efforts redoubled, likely in response to Kat's latter statement.

'All right, fine,' she says with a shrug, prompting Bards to kiss Kat on the cheek in celebration and make her giggle. Jess turns to me. 'Guessing you're not coming?'

'I can't, but have a good one,' I say, stepping forward to give her a hug. Bards releases Kat for a moment so I can hug her too, whispering in her ear, 'Don't do anything I wouldn't.'

'That doesn't leave me many options,' she replies.

I roll my eyes, but it's a fair comment, the sort that makes my heart sink. I shake it off.

'I'll walk you home, Dawson,' Harley announces, looking up from his phone.

'What?' Bards balks at the offer. 'Harley, you're coming with us.'

'I'll walk Billie home and then I'll come back out for the party,' Harley tells him breezily. 'Her house is next to mine; it's a short walk. I won't be long.'

'You *really* don't need to do that,' I say to Harley, frowning at him.

'See? You don't need to do that,' Bards echoes.

'It's late; you're not walking home alone,' Harley tells me firmly.

'Thanks, Harley,' Jess says, smiling at him.

'No, I'll be fine,' I say through gritted teeth, my eyes widening at her, annoyed that she's encouraging him. 'Like you say, Harley, it's a short walk and I can call my brother on the way if that makes you feel better, but I—'

'See you guys at the party,' Harley calls back over his shoulder to the others, already walking in the direction of our street. 'Come on, Dawson, keep up.'

As the other three wave goodbye and stroll off in the opposite direction, I reluctantly fall into step with Harley. For a minute or so, we remain in an awkward silence, walking side by side.

'Thank you,' I blurt out, unable to take it any more. 'For offering to walk me home, I mean. But you should go to your party.'

'I will afterwards,' he replies simply, shoving his hands in his pockets. 'So, tell me, Dawson, what are your plans for this summer now we're free of school?'

'You *know* my plans.'

He gives me a strange look. 'Considering we rarely talk and I haven't hacked into your phone to study your calendar, funnily enough, I don't know your plans.'

'Wimbledon,' I say, raising my eyebrows at him. 'You know, that big tennis tournament that happens every summer? The greatest grass tournament in the sport; the championships that—'

'Yeah, I'm familiar,' he says, the corners of his mouth twitching upwards.

'So, then, you know my plans,' I say, pleased to have made my point. 'Wimbledon this summer before I go to the University of East London in September.'

'Okay, but Wimbledon only happens across one week, right? At the start of July?'

'Yeah, the junior tournament takes place during the second week of the Wimbledon Championships. The week before, we'll be playing in the ITF J300 Roehampton Tournament, which is on grass as well. Good practice in the lead-up to Wimbledon, and we'll get a chance to see what our competition is like.'

'Sure. That's ... two weeks total. One week at the end of June for the doubles tournament at the Roehampton courts; one week at the beginning of July for Wimbledon,' Harley sums up, looking at me expectantly. 'So, what else?'

'What do you mean, "what else"?'

'I mean, what are you doing for the rest of the summer?' he explains with a pinch of exasperation. 'What else have you got planned before UEL? I get the feeling you're big on plans and schedules.'

'I've got nothing else planned. That's all I care about.' He halts in his tracks. I come to a stop myself, turning to frown at him. 'What?'

'You have nothing else planned all summer?' he says in disbelief, strolling forward again. 'Like ... *nothing*?'

'That's quite a big thing to have going on.'

'Yeah, but it's not like ...' He trails off and I glance over at him to see his forehead creased in confusion. 'Dawson, you just finished school.'

'So?'

'So, this is the Summer of Freedom!'

'No one calls it that.'

'*I* call it that,' he emphasizes, amusement flashing in his eyes. 'We're finally free of exams, heading out into the big wide world, and we're given one last summer to let loose before we have to grow up and take on responsibility. I'm telling you now, Dawson, you need to take advantage of that.'

'What do you want me to say? That I'm going to spend my summer going to loads of parties and embarrassing myself?' I suggest scornfully, unimpressed.

'Yes!' he exclaims, laughing as we turn the corner onto our street. 'That's exactly what I'm saying. I think embarrassing yourself is underrated. I reckon a lot of people, when they're older, look back and wish they'd spent more time embarrassing themselves.'

'How profound,' I murmur, rolling my eyes. '*Some* of us

want to do more with our lives than waste them at parties and fucking around.'

He slows as we reach our houses. 'Is that what you think of me, then? That I'm just ... wasting my life "fucking around"?'

'I didn't say that.'

'You implied it.'

We've come to a stop on the pavement next to the end of the fence that divides our homes. I turn slowly to face him. His lips are curved in a playful smile, his eyes searching mine. Even when he's being insulted, Harley seems to find it funny.

I don't think there's one thing that he takes seriously.

'I don't know you,' I say flatly, glancing at his house. I can hear music playing in the front room and see a silhouette of someone dancing around on their own in there. I think that must be his mum. His dad's car isn't in the driveway. 'But being your neighbour, I have been able to get a glimpse into your life.'

'And what *glimpse* have you got?'

'Enough of one to know that you and I are very different.'

'In what way?'

'Harley—'

'In your opinion, why are we so different?' he asks sternly. 'I know what I think the answer to that question is. I want to know what *you* think.'

I exhale, throwing my hands up. 'I don't know. You ... go

out a lot. I've seen you with a lot of girls, always a different one ... I guess we have different priorities.'

'Fucking hell,' he says, smiling in disbelief as he looks down on the ground, shaking his head. He lifts it to bring his eyes to meet mine. 'A lot of judgement from the posh girl next door who never puts a toe out of line. I didn't know you were spying on me.'

'I'm not!' I protest, heat flushing up my neck. 'And I'm not posh.'

'You may have been watching me, Dawson, but I've been watching you, too,' he continues brazenly, fixing me with a searing gaze that makes my cheeks burn. 'You have no time for anyone or anything but tennis. I don't think I've ever seen you with a guy ... Oh, wait –' he breaks into a grin – 'there was one. The guy from the tennis club. The posh one who fawns all over you. You can see the saliva drooling from his mouth when he looks at you longingly ... I have to be careful I don't slip in the pool of it when he comes off the court.'

I narrow my eyes at him as he stands there, amused at his own joke.

'Caleb does not drool,' I say crossly.

Harley clicks his fingers. 'That's the one: Caleb. I'm surprised you had a thing with him. I'd have thought you'd have better taste. A bit up his own arse, isn't he?'

'No, he's not.' I bristle, even though it's true, but it's

infuriating for Harley to be right. 'Caleb is ... He's nice. We weren't right for each other, that's all ... Anyway, it's none of your business. And what's your obsession with everyone else being "posh"? You've said it about Caleb, about me – we live on the same street, Harley.'

'Same street, different worlds,' he argues, unfazed. 'We went to different schools. You and I both know that the only reason I'm a member of your fancy tennis club is because my uncle works there and he sorted me out. And you and your friends are prim and proper – you've made it clear tonight that you don't think mine are good enough for them. You look down your nose at me, Billie Dawson.'

'I think that chip on your shoulder is impeding your vision, Harley. I couldn't give a shit about where we went to school or who your friends are ...' I hesitate. 'Although I admit that, yeah, Bards isn't good enough for Kat, but no one on this planet is good enough for her. She's my best friend, so I have every right to say that and no one will ever change my mind. Does that make you feel better?'

'Very sweet,' he remarks, leaning an arm on the fence and looking me up and down. 'Here I was thinking that you weren't the sentimental type. You continue to surprise me.'

'What, you think that because I work hard, I don't have any feelings? You had me pinned as the icy-cold bitch.' I sigh. 'You continue to disappoint me.'

'*Aha!*' He straightens triumphantly, pointing his finger at me. 'There, you admit it. You do see me as a disappointment, now and before.'

Growing too frustrated to continue this pointless conversation, I reach into my bag for my keys. 'I'm going inside.'

'Wait,' he says, reaching out to grab my hand.

When I look up in surprise, I find he's taken a small step towards me, closing the gap between us. His eyes lock with mine and suddenly my mouth feels very dry, tingles running up and down my arms.

'What?' I ask, my voice a little hoarse.

His brow furrows as he gazes down at me.

'Nothing ... Goodnight, Billie Dawson.'

The way he's looking at me is so intense, it's making my heart rate quicken.

Forcing myself to step back from him, I turn around and march up the pathway to my house, fumbling with my keys as I unlock the door and shut it after me without glancing back. I lean against the door for a moment to steady my breath.

Steeling myself, I creep into our living room, purposefully not turning on the lights so that I can peer out the window without him seeing. He's still there at the fence between our houses, smiling to himself. He must have watched me walk all the way to the door. Scuffing the toe of his shoe on the pavement, he puts his hands in his pockets and turns round to walk away, sauntering back from where we came, off to the party where he'll be surrounded by girls desperate to win his attention.

And he'll look at them in the exact same way he looked at me.

CHAPTER FIVE

A week later, I knock loudly on Tom's bedroom door. When I hear the muffled sound of him reluctantly saying 'come in' into his pillow, I swing the door open and march in, moving to tower over him in bed with my hands on my hips.

'What is going on with you?' I demand to know as he groans, turning away from me and pulling the duvet over his head. I reach to pull it back. 'Do you know what time it is?'

'Time to sleep,' he mutters, eyes firmly shut.

'It's eleven in the morning!'

'I'm having a lie-in,' he huffs, nestling his head into the pillow.

'You've been having a lie-in every day this week. And you're napping all the time.' I sit down, shoving his legs over so I can perch on the side of the bed. 'What's wrong?'

'Nothing's wrong.'

'Something's wrong,' I counter, prodding his shoulder. 'Talk to me.'

He rolls over onto his back. 'Nothing's wrong, Billie. I'm tired, that's all.'

'Why are you so tired? Are you not sleeping? Is something bothering you? Is there something on your mind you want to talk about?'

He rubs his forehead. 'Nope. I'm fine.'

'All week you've been too tired to go jogging or work out. You've barely made it to practice.' I give him a look. 'Nick and I are worried about you.'

'Well, don't be,' he says, stifling a yawn. 'I promise, Billie – there's nothing to worry about. I'm feeling a bit run down. I've got a bit of a cold or something.'

'You've been feeling run down for a while,' I observe, biting my lip. 'Tom, I think you should go to a doctor.'

He snorts at the idea. 'Don't be dramatic, Bills. I'm allowed a couple of lie-ins. Not all of us function a million miles per hour like you and the Duracell Bunny.'

'You've said your muscles are aching.'

'Because I've been forced to work out every day of my life and never get time off to relax,' he grumbles, moving to sit himself up, plumping up his pillow behind him before he slumps back against it. 'Maybe we've been pushing things too hard.'

I frown at him. He looks paler than usual, dark circles forming under his eyes. 'You haven't been eating well this week. It's like you're not hungry any more, and yesterday in practice, you kept needing to sit down and—'

'Christ, Billie, you're not Mum, so stop pretending to be,' he snaps.

I press my lips together, eyes dropping to the floor. He sighs, reaching up to rub the back of his neck.

'Sorry,' he says quietly, 'I didn't mean to ... I know you're looking out for me.' He drops his hand to his lap. 'I'm *fine*. Don't you ever want a break from everything? I think my body is trying to tell me to slow down.'

'But Roehampton is around the corner. We can't slow down. Not now.'

'I know.' He nods, his eyes glazed with exhaustion. 'I don't know what's been going on. The pressure ... it can get to me.'

'You're the best tennis player I know,' I say, surprised at his admission. 'You don't need to worry about pressure. Everyone knows how brilliant you are.'

He looks over at Rufus, chilling in his enclosure.

'Tom?' I prompt after a while of him just staring at the other side of the room.

'Yeah, sorry,' he says, dragging his eyes back to me and fixing a smile. Peeling his duvet off his body, he forces himself up out of bed as though it's taking a lot of effort. 'I'll go shower and then let's get to the courts. I'll make up for missing training this morning.'

'If you need a break, then we should—'

'I've had one,' he interrupts, plodding out of his room to the bathroom. 'I'm ready now.'

I'm at the net, crouching low, spinning my tennis racket in my hand, waiting for Tom to serve from the baseline behind me. Nick is the other end of the court, ready to return.

I hate that Tom won't talk to me, that he's keeping something from me. If something is worrying him to this extent that he's lost all motivation for tennis training, then it's something big. The only positive is that I've had to work harder to cover our butts on the court, so while his performance is dipping, my fitness is rocketing.

I hear the three soft thuds as he bounces the ball before he serves.

Nick bends his knees, ready to return.

I wait to hear the sound of Tom's racket swish through the air and the satisfying crack of the ball smacking against the strings as he sends it over the net, but nothing comes.

Nick slowly straightens, peering at my brother in concern. 'Tom?'

Spinning round, I see him stumbling to the back of the court so he can lean his weight against the fence, dropping his racket to the ground with a clatter.

'Tom!' I cry, racing over to him and seeing beads of sweat dripping down his face.

'Something's wrong,' he says in a raspy voice, his skin pale, his eyelids drooping.

He collapses to the ground before I can say I told him so.

I hate hospitals. I hate the bright lights, the potent smell of chemicals and bleach, the high-pitched squeak my trainers make on the floor, the background noise of machines beeping and people coughing, the hard plastic chairs of the waiting room, the weak coffee of the machines. I hate that all of it reminds me of Mum.

'Why don't you sit down, Billie?' Nick suggests gently as I pace back and forth. 'I'm sure we'll get some news soon.'

I wonder if he's partly saying that because of the incessant squeak of my trainers.

My hands clasped behind my back, I lean against the wall opposite him, my leg shaking impatiently. Dad is on his way from the office. I felt an irrational stab of guilt when I had to phone him to ask him to come here. It will remind him of Mum, too.

She always raved about the hospital. 'Yeah, the food isn't great,' she'd say with a laugh, 'but the people are wonderful.' All the doctors and nurses couldn't do enough for her: they made her laugh; they were soothing when she was in pain.

'Hospitals have to be clinical,' she'd tell me and Tom when we worried about her being stuck there, 'but the people within them aren't. They've seen it all and they won't let it break their spirit. Talk about courage.'

I know that hospitals and their staff are amazing, but every time I walk into one, I relive the consuming feeling of dread that would overwhelm me back when Mum was sick. The fear that I would walk in through those doors with her, but walk out of them without her.

'Why do you think it's taking so long?' I ask Nick, trying to distract myself from thoughts of Mum and the anxiety of what's happening to Tom.

'There's a queue of people that probably needed to be seen before him, and they need to be thorough,' he replies calmly. 'He wasn't a serious case. He fainted, that's all. Billie, he's going to be *fine*.'

'This is my fault,' I admit quietly, a lump caught in my throat. 'He said he needed a break, that he was pushing too hard. Now this.'

Nick doesn't say anything, reaching up to put a comforting hand on my shoulder.

'Billie!' Dad's voice echoes around the waiting room as he bursts through the doors and spots me, rushing over. 'How is he? Have you heard anything?'

I'm about to say what I know – which isn't much – when a doctor approaches us.

'Tom Dawson's family?' she checks.

'Yes, I'm his father,' Dad says, turning to her, panicked.

'He's okay now; you can come see him,' she says with a comforting smile, gesturing for us to follow her down the corridor to his ward. I scurry behind Dad, desperately trying to listen to everything she says. 'He was dehydrated and he tells me he's been experiencing fatigue recently, the combination of which would have caused him to faint when he was overexerting himself by playing sport.'

'What's wrong with him? Is it serious?' Dad asks as she comes to a halt outside the ward. 'Should we be worried?'

'His glands are swollen. It could just be a case of a sore throat and feeling a bit under the weather,' she explains. 'But he says the tiredness has been affecting him for a while, so I've run some blood tests just in case, to rule out other illnesses. We'll be in touch with the results. In the meantime, he should rest. I see from his records that he's very active.'

'He's a tennis player,' Dad tells her. 'He's due to play in Junior Wimbledon soon.'

'It's important that he takes it easy for a while and doesn't risk dehydration,' she says sternly. 'He needs to avoid that level of training and exercise.'

'So ... no tennis,' my dad checks, his eyes filled with concern.

'For now, no tennis,' she confirms. 'And definitely no Wimbledon.'

CHAPTER SIX

'What is the big deal?' Tom says to me a couple of days later, curled up under the blanket on the sofa, his eyes shining with excitement. 'Nick's right! You could still win this thing.'

'No,' I say adamantly, passing him a glass of water. 'I'm not playing the tournament without you.'

'Why not?' he asks, rolling his eyes as I gesture for him to drink more. He takes a couple of glugs and passes back the glass before I slump down on the sofa next to him. 'I *want* you to play. You know how guilty I feel about all of this?'

'I've told you that I—'

'You can say you don't mind a million times, Billie – I'm still going to feel bad,' he cuts in, giving me a look. 'I know how much you wanted it.'

My eyes drop to my lap. 'You wanted it, too.'

From the armchair opposite, Nick clears his throat. 'You don't have to make a decision now, Billie. I was dropping by mainly to check in on how you were getting on, Tom, and I thought it worth mentioning that there's still time to apply for the tournament with a different doubles partner. *Just* time. The cut-off date is end of play tomorrow.'

'Just because I have to bow out, doesn't mean you have to,' Tom presses, nudging my leg with his toe. 'I don't know whether you've heard Dad mention it, but I do already have a Wimbledon win under my belt.'

I can't help but laugh. He breaks into a satisfied smile at my reaction.

'Come on, Billie,' he encourages. 'Think about it.'

But I don't *want* to think about it. That's what Tom doesn't get. I don't want to play doubles tennis with anyone but him. He's my twin; he's my favourite person to play tennis with; our game complements each other's; we grew up on the court *together*. That's why we're so hard to beat, and that's why people thought we might have a chance of winning the tournament this year.

Tom knows I'm worried about him, that waiting for the results from his tests is torturous for us all, but he also knows how much this tournament means to me. He knows why my eyes were so red and puffy this morning. So when Nick arrived at our house about half an hour ago to propose the idea that I consider playing with a different partner, Tom has been nothing but optimistic about it.

I can feel both of them watching me intently as I ponder the idea.

'Tom, there's no way I can learn how to play with someone new in such a short time,' I say, heaving a sigh. 'Roehampton is less than three weeks away. We've been playing together all our lives. We know each other's strengths and tactics inside out. We work brilliantly together. That's just not going to be the same with anyone else.'

'You never know, Billie,' Nick reasons.

'A new partner might even bring out strengths you didn't even know you had,' Tom adds excitedly. 'You've never thought to consider anyone else, and that might have been holding you back. Mixing it up a bit could be a good thing.'

'No way. You're the best player at the club.'

'There are others who could be as good,' Nick tells me, finishing the cup of tea I made him earlier and placing it down on the side table. 'Especially if they had you helping them, Billie. With your focus and drive, and a disciplined training regime in the lead-up to the tournament, I think there are a couple of people who might be able to match you.'

I frown, biting my lip.

The idea of playing with anyone but Tom seems alien to me. But the idea of still having the chance to play this tournament is sparking a warm flicker of hope in my stomach.

'I don't know,' I mutter. 'There's a lot that could go wrong. It might not work. A new doubles partner this late in the game could be completely disastrous.'

'Or, it could be the start of something,' Nick adds, looking at me hopefully.

'Billie,' Tom begins, leaning forward, 'for once in your life, *take a risk.*'

I stare back at him, my heart rate quickening. 'You really think I should do this?'

'Yes,' he says, no hesitation. 'I really do.'

I find myself nodding. 'All right, then,' I say, as Tom breaks into a grin. I turn to Nick to find him beaming at me. 'Who did you have in mind?'

THWACK!

I yelp as the ball hits me in the back of the head.

'Oh, bugger it!' Caleb cries, running over as I straighten, rubbing the sore spot where I can already feel a bump forming. 'Are you okay? I have a very powerful serve – that must have hurt a *lot.*'

'Fine, I'm fine.' I wince, my eyes watering as I wave him back to the baseline.

'Fuck's sake,' he says crossly, hitting the side of his trainer with his racket. 'I can't believe I did that *again.*'

'Me neither,' I mutter under my breath, shooting Nick a glare.

Grimacing, Nick looks as broken as I feel. Caleb is the second person we've trialled today as a potential partner for me, and he's turning out to be even more useless than the first.

The first guy was Asher, a sixteen-year-old rising star from a sports club nearby. He's a brilliant singles player, who is keen to play doubles too, but it became clear early on that we didn't match up – he controlled the court on his terms and was baffled at the idea of sharing the play. At one point, the ball was clearly coming my way and he yelled, 'MINE!' before throwing himself across the court at it, taking my feet out from under me as he lunged for the ball. Nick agreed that he didn't have the mindset for doubles and he'd rather not risk my new partner injuring me before the tournament had even begun.

There are few people with a high enough ITF ranking to qualify alongside me who are local and aren't already partnered up with someone else, so it's not like I have many options. Caleb feels like my last hope, and I knew as soon as he walked onto the court that it wasn't going to work out. I've already had to talk him through the tantrum he had when he messed up a return. I could see the pair we're playing against, Scarlett and Evan, trying not to snigger as he yelled and stomped at the baseline. Scarlett threw me a sympathetic look, which told me all I needed to know – as his usual partner, she's clearly suffered this a few times.

I hear Caleb mutter to himself, 'Get the ball over the fucking net, you twat,' as he prepares to serve again, and I try to stealthily move myself as much out of the way as possible, hoping to protect my poor little head without making him feel worse. He hits it much softer this time, and the ball drops onto their side of the net, before Evan returns it with a beautiful forehand spin. It's Caleb's ball and he pelts towards it, swinging wildly at the ball and sending it smashing into the top of the net.

'*Fuuuuuck!*' he cries, tipping his head back.

'Love–fifteen,' Nick says grimly.

Straightening, I say, 'Don't worry about it,' to Caleb through a fixed smile, but he's too busy hissing expletives at himself to hear me. My heart is sinking and I can tell from Nick's expression that he's thinking the same as me: it's no use. This isn't working.

'Unlucky, Caleb,' calls out a familiar voice behind us.

Harley has wandered over with his racket over his shoulder, his eyes flashing with intrigue. He must have a lesson with Nick after this. *Brilliant*. Just what Caleb needs, some idiot taunting him. I shoot Harley a warning look as he remains where he is, leaning against the fence at the back of the court, before clearing my throat and smiling widely at Caleb as he picks up two balls for his next serve.

'You've got this,' I tell him.

He ignores me, rage etched into his forehead. Turning back to face our opponents, I crouch into position, trying to push away the negative thoughts. Caleb's first serve is way too forceful, landing beyond the baseline at the other end and bouncing against the fencing around the court. I don't react, willing Caleb to stay calm and collected, and doing my best not to picture the smug smile I know is on Harley's face right now.

Scarlett readies herself for his second serve, moving in closer. I know that will annoy Caleb and I hear him huff behind me. Gripping the handle of my racket, I bend my knees, ready on the balls of my feet. His serve is weak, but it goes in, landing with a gentle bounce in front of Scarlett, who returns it long and wide across the court back to Caleb.

Out of the corner of my eye, I see him go for it and fall, tripping over his own feet and landing in a heap on the ground. He cries out in pain as the ball bounces over his head.

'Mine!' Harley says, leaping into action and running forward to hit the ball back.

I watch in total confusion as the ball soars past me, landing in play at the edge of the doubles sideline.

Taken slightly off guard, Scarlett just about makes it, whacking the ball back our way with a clumsy backhand. It loops over my head diagonally across the court. Harley is there, sending it soaring back to their baseline with a smooth and powerful backhand.

'Harley, what are you doing?' I yell, as Caleb hobbles away from the court.

Evan meets Harley's backhand with a good volley, the ball zipping past me down the centre of the court.

'In case you didn't notice,' Harley replies, rotating his

body and swinging his racket back as the ball bounces, before playing a beautiful forehand back down their centre line, 'I'm saving your butt!'

'Oh *please*!' I huff, moving into position as Scarlett manages a lob back.

I wait as the ball drops towards me and then I smash it with power and precision into the open space between Evan and Scarlett to win the point.

I spin round to face Harley with my hands on my hips.

'We're in the middle of something here,' I tell him, flicking my ponytail back over my shoulder.

'From where I'm standing, you're down a partner,' he counters, nodding to where Caleb is sitting to the side of the court, examining his ankle.

'Fifteen–all,' Nick calls out. 'Harley, your serve.'

'Hang on a second!' I stare at Nick as Harley triumphantly goes to collect a couple of balls, moving to the right side of the court. 'I'm supposed to be playing with Caleb.'

'He's injured,' Nick replies, his brow furrowed, his eyes fixed on Harley.

'Then we should give up and stop the game.'

'I'd move if I were you, Dawson,' Harley calls out, stepping up to the baseline and bouncing a ball in front of him as Evan prepares to return on the other side of the net.

'What are you ... ? Coach, this is pointless!' I appeal to Nick, but he shrugs.

Throwing my hands up in exasperation, I jog across the court, but I'm not happy about it. Harley is going to turn this into something silly, something trivial.

My jaw locked with tension, I bend my knees and wait for him to hit me in the back on purpose or something as a joke. Surprisingly, I see a blur of yellow go zipping past me over the net, landing in the service box and flying out of reach of Evan's stretched-out racket.

Ace.

'Thirty–fifteen,' Nick declares, stroking his chin.

'You see that, Dawson? Not bad, huh,' Harley cries, winking at me as he catches the ball that Evan chucks back to him for the next serve.

I narrow my eyes at him as I move the opposite way across the court and get into position.

'Ah, one of these days I'll impress you,' he calls after me.

'Unlikely.'

He chuckles and then falls silent. I hear two thuds against the ground before the swish of his racket. The ball flies past me, bouncing on the service line towards Scarlett. It's a powerful serve, but her racket is there to deflect the ball back across court, where it lands softly on the singles sideline of the left service box. Harley races forward to reach it and I naturally drop back to cover the baseline now he's moved up to the net. He returns the ball with a smooth backhand slice. Evan can't reach it, but Scarlett is doing everything she can to get there, pelting forward at full speed. She just about gets it, sending it up and over.

'Got it!' I call out to Harley as the ball flies in a loop over his head.

'Yep,' he replies, getting swiftly out my way so I can move round the ball into position before hitting a winning forehand right down the centre of the court, through the middle of Evan and Scarlett, who both look too stunned to try for it.

'Forty–fifteen,' Nick says.

'You know, it's nice to play a game alongside you again, Dawson – it's been too long,' Harley comments as we drift past one another, him coming back to the baseline, me returning to the net. 'Gives us the chance to talk. I enjoyed our date at Rambler's the other day.'

'That was *not* a date.'

'You bought me a drink; I walked you home,' he reels off, selecting a ball for his serve. 'Sounds like a date to me.'

'If that's your idea of a date, Harley, then I feel sorry for the girls who've had to suffer them,' I say, bending my knees as I face the net, rotating the handle of my racket in my grip.

He laughs. 'Fair point. You know what? On our second date, *I'll* buy the drink. And you feel free to walk *me* home. You might get lucky and be invited in for a nightcap.'

Without turning back to give him the satisfaction of a response, I roll my eyes.

He bounces the ball and serves down the line to Evan's

backhand. It's such a powerful serve, it catches Evan on the back foot and he returns it clumsily, sending it soaring right at me. It takes very little effort for me to send it smashing down on their side of the court.

Neither of them bother to move for it.

'Game, set and *match*,' Nick says with a laugh, clapping his hands.

Straightening, I give a sharp nod of approval and then spin round to find Harley jogging towards me, holding up his hand for a high-five. I tap my hand lightly against his and before I can draw it away, he grabs it, holding it in his strong grip.

'We make a good team, Dawson,' he remarks, his eyes gleaming at me.

'Life is full of surprises. You play all right, when you want to.'

'A compliment! From you?' He quirks a brow. 'Life really *is* full of surprises.'

'Brilliant, you two,' Nick says as he approaches us. 'Problem solved.'

I pull my hand free from Harley's warm grasp. 'Sorry?'

'Looks like we've found your new doubles partner, Billie,' Nick says, folding his arms and grinning at Harley. 'Wimbledon, here we come!'

My jaw drops open. I look back at Harley, who looks as bewildered as I feel.

You have got to be kidding me.

CHAPTER SEVEN

This is a terrible idea. A really terrible idea. The *worst*. But Nick refuses to listen or see sense. He is completely deluded if he thinks there's a chance this might work.

'Not him,' I say, confronting Nick in the club after practice. 'It can't be him.'

'He has a high enough ITF ranking to qualify, and you two played out there like you've been playing together for years,' Nick points out, his eyes lit up with hope as if he's genuinely excited by the idea. 'I don't know why I didn't think of him before.'

'I do! Because he has zero motivation! He won't want to be a part of this.'

'He seemed very enthusiastic to play with you,' he says with a hint of a knowing smile. 'Think about it, Billie: your styles complement each other. He's a brilliant player with a stylish flair; you're an outstanding player with grit and ambition. His baseline work is great, and we all know your aggression at the net. It's a great match.'

'It is *not* a great match,' I reply tensely. 'We've played together before, *remember*?'

Nick looks down at the floor. He knows what I'm talking about: the charity tournament the club organized three summers back when Harley and I were randomly paired together. We got through to the final – but he didn't bother to show up that day. I was left hopelessly waiting for him at the side of the court until our competitors were declared the winners of the tournament by default. It was humiliating and disappointing.

Harley purposefully avoided me for days after that, and then when I finally bumped into him outside his house and demanded an apology, he shrugged and said he'd had to miss the final for 'personal reasons'. I knew it was bullshit and I learned a valuable lesson. Harley Pierce is not someone you can rely on.

'That was years ago. Things have changed,' Nick says weakly.

'Not from where I'm standing. If anything, he's more irresponsible now. Nick, this needs to be an intense training programme. Do you think he's going to take it seriously?'

'Yes,' Nick says, looking pensive. 'I think if anyone can whip Harley into shape, it's you. I also think this could be good for you, too.'

I blink at him. 'Excuse me?'

'He makes you play better.'

'*What?*'

'When you were playing together today, you played better,' he repeats firmly, looking me right in the eye. 'He improves your game and you *definitely* improve his. It's like you're both trying your best to be good enough for the other one.'

'That is *not* what it's like!'

He sighs. 'Billie, you're just going to have to trust me on this.'

'Nick, I know he's your nephew, so I don't want to ... upset you, but Harley and I ... we don't get on. Okay? We clash in every possible way. Even if our styles work together, our personalities don't. We don't like each other.'

'Who says you have to like each other to win? All you have to do is respect each other's game – you may not admit it, but I can tell you think he's good – and communicate well. We have time to work on the communication.'

'Nick, you're not hearing me. This is a bad idea.'

He places his hands on my shoulders. 'All I'm asking is you give him a chance, Billie. You might be surprised.'

I exhale, pressing my lips together. Nick folds his arms, raising his eyebrows at me.

'And honestly, at this stage, what other options do you have?' he adds.

As much as I hate that he's right ... he's right. No one else even comes close to being a good fit. It's either Harley Pierce or no Wimbledon at all.

'Fine,' I say quietly, closing my eyes. 'I'll give him a chance.'

'Good,' Nick says, his eyes drifting over my shoulder.

I turn around to see Harley sauntering through from the men's locker rooms, his hair wet and dishevelled from the shower, his tennis bag over his shoulder. As he approaches, I feel unnerved by how good he smells, inhaling a waft of his musky sandalwood cologne.

'What's the verdict?' he asks Nick.

'She's game if you are,' comes the reply, while I keep my eyes fixed on my shoes.

'I'm game, Coach,' Harley confirms. 'Get that application in. We're good to go.'

Nick pats me on the arm. 'I'm excited for this new pairing. Let's talk things through tomorrow, but for now, go home and rest up.'

As Nick leaves, Harley turns his attention to me.

'Hey, I've been meaning to ask how your brother is,' he says, his question taking me by surprise. 'How's he doing?'

'He's fine, thanks,' I say, eyeing him up suspiciously.

He raises his eyebrows at me. 'What? I'm not allowed to care about your brother? I don't know him well, but whenever I see him around, he seems cool. I'm sorry he's ill.'

My brow furrowed, I nod, chewing on the inside of my cheek. I don't really know what to say to that. Harley doesn't seem to mind.

'So, looks like we're going to be seeing a lot more of each other this summer than we thought,' he says, nudging me with his elbow, his light teasing tone much more in line with the Harley I know. I can be annoyed at him again now. 'Talk to me about the social scene of the junior tournament at Wimbledon. I'm guessing it's pretty hot, right? Lots of athletes looking to let off a bit of steam . . .'

I narrow my eyes at him. 'This is just another joke to you, isn't it.'

He shrugs. 'No. But it's the junior contest, right? Not the real thing. So we'll work hard, but I'm thinking we play hard, too. I reckon we—'

That's it. My blood boils over and I round on him, jabbing my finger into his broad chest, which is amazingly solid.

'Listen,' I say in a fierce, low tone that prompts a flash of fear to cross his expression already, and I haven't even said my bit yet, 'you better get your arse in gear for this competition and work hard. There is no way in *hell* that I'm going to let you get in the way or fuck up something that I have worked so hard to be a part of. If you say you're going to do this, then you better show up.'

'Whoa.' He takes a step back. 'I see what this is about.'

'Good. You get that this is important to me.'

'No, I mean I can see where all this –' he gestures to me – '*anger* is coming from.'

'What are you talking about?'

'That charity tournament when we were fifteen,' he says, nodding slowly as though he's figured out a mysterious puzzle. 'You're still mad about it.'

'What?'

'I get it, it was bad and I should have messaged, but really, Billie?' He tilts his head at me. 'It was three years ago.'

'And I'm over it,' I say, growing flustered. 'I don't care about that.'

'I think you do. It's okay. I can see that you're the type of person to hold a grudge. A little pathetic when it's from so long ago and over a silly tennis competition that meant ... nothing, considering the charity still received all the money – but, hey, you do you. If you need to vent your frustration about it, go ahead. It's been building all these years.'

'It has not!'

'I'm kind of honoured,' he says, his lips curving into a mischievous smile. 'It makes me feel good to know that I've been under your skin all this time.'

'Oh my god, that is not ... *argh*!' I run my fingers through my hair. 'You are so *annoying*.'

'See, the lads told me you were impenetrable, but here I am, on your mind day and night.'

Closing my eyes, I take a deep breath through my nose to collect myself. I won't let him get to me. *I will not let him get to me.*

'Hey, Dawson, are you by any chance fantasizing about me

right now?' he whispers in a low voice, dipping his head close to me.

When my eyes flutter open, his face is inches from mine. Holding his gaze, I don't flinch. I'm back in control now.

'Oh, Harley,' I say, smiling sweetly, 'you are the last person in the world I would fantasize about. A complete lack of ambition doesn't exactly do it for me.'

He draws back, his eyes dropping to the floor. 'Ouch. You've got me there, Dawson.'

'I need to know whether you really want to do this,' I say calmly, my smile fading. 'If you can't take this seriously, then don't waste my time. I won't let you humiliate me.'

He glances up, looking stung. 'I would never do that to you.'

'You've done it before,' I snap back. 'Yeah, it was three years ago. And, yeah, it wasn't exactly a contest that mattered in the bigger picture – but it mattered to me, and I won't forget how small you made me feel that day, standing at the court in front of all those people, waiting around for a partner who never came.'

A muscle in Harley's jaw twitches.

'This contest *does* matter,' I continue, watching him carefully as he avoids eye contact. 'Maybe not to others, but it matters to me. It really matters. In fact, right now, it's everything to me. So if you can't bring a hundred and ten per cent to this, if you are going to let me down further down the line, then please, *please* spare me the pain and wasted time and bow out now.'

He exhales, mustering the courage to look at me. 'I said I was game. I meant it.'

My eyes search his, desperate to find the sincerity that I hope is there.

'Okay, good. I'll see you tomorrow at practice then,' I conclude.

His jaw tense, he stalks past me, and I only just manage to stumble back in time before I'm hit in the shoulder by his tennis bag. Shaking his head as he approaches the door, I watch as he pauses, gripping the handle. He turns back to me.

'Did you say this contest means *everything* to you?' he checks.

I nod, lifting my chin. 'Yes. It does.'

'Fuck me, Dawson, you really need to get a life.'

He turns and swings open the door, sauntering through it, chuckling as he goes.

Floored by his brutal comment, I close my eyes in despair. *We're doomed.*

CHAPTER EIGHT

Melrose's finest 🌿🖤

> **Jess**
> Good luck this morning, Billie!
> First proper practice with Harley, right?

> **Billie**
> Thanks, Jess
> Bit nervous

> **Jess**
> He's the one who should be nervous
> I hope he's ready for what's coming
> Seriously though, I have faith

> **Billie**
> Faith in me or in him?

Jess
Both of you!

Kat
Girls, I'm dying
I actually think this is it
This is the end

Jess
I take it last night was fun?

Kat
Death by tequila

> **Billie**
> Ouch
> Who were you out with?

Kat
Bards and his mates

Jess
Again?!

> **Billie**
> Isn't that the fourth time this week?

Kat
What can I say
That boy knows what he's doing
If you know what I mean
Do you know what I mean?
You KNOW what I mean

Jess
Yeah, thanks, Kat
I think we've got it

Kat
Makes a change to be with someone with a bit of experience

Anyway, they'll be with you in a bit, Bills

> **Billie**
> Who will?

Kat
Bards and Harley

> Bards is going to drive him to the courts
> He's getting ready to go

Billie
Wait, what??
You're with Harley??

Kat
Yeah I'm at Bards's house
Harley slept on the sofa last night
Or passed out there, I should say

Jess
Uh-oh
That can't be good

Billie
Kat, we're meant to be on the court in FIVE MINUTES

I'm messaging from the locker room!
He's not even here yet??

Kat
Oh
Uh, no, he's still here
He's standing in front of me drinking a coffee
He's topless
And I'm going to throw it out there
He is HOT
Billie, you are SO lucky
You should get him to train topless

> **Billie**
> I don't believe this

Kat
You want me to take a picture?

> **Billie**
> NO
> I mean, I can't believe he's so late!

Kat
He's asked me to tell you that he's on his way

Billie
IS he on his way?
Or is he just saying that?

Kat
He's just saying that
But he will be soon
Bards needs to find his car keys
I should probably help look
But I'm too hungover to move
Bards is getting cross at me

Billie
I knew this would happen
I told Nick this would happen

Jess
Maybe when he arrives he'll play amazingly
And you'll forget all your troubles

Billie
Something tells me that's not how it's going to go

Jess
I don't know
He seems like the type to be able to pull it off

Billie
You don't know him
Kat, is he in the car yet?

Kat
The boys are still hunting for the keys

Billie
I'm going to kill him

Jess
Could be worse
He could not show at all

Billie
I don't know if that's worse
Sounds great to me

Jess
You don't mean that

> **Billie**
> It's our first training session
> He can't even show up on time
> Or sober

> **Jess**
> Just focus on Wimbledon
> You've worked so hard for this, Bills
> Don't give up yet

> **Kat**
> Jess is right
> Harley really wants to be there
> He's searching for these keys
> I should get up and help

> OMG
> Guess what?!
> I was sitting on the car keys the whole time!
> Lucky I decided to get up
> The boys are on their way! X

The car door swings open and Harley practically crawls out of it.

Nick and I stand by the fencing, eyes on the car park, looking on unimpressed as Harley rakes his fingers through his unruly mane of hair, Wayfarers on, shoulders slumped. As he goes to close the passenger door, it seems as though it's a real effort, and when it slams shut, he jumps at the loud bang it makes, groaning and rubbing his head.

'Oh, Harley,' Nick mutters under his breath, his eyebrows knitted together.

I'm too angry to say anything. I'm already in a bad mood because I'm so worried about Tom. He could barely get out of bed this morning, he's so tired. The last thing I needed was for Harley to let me down today.

'Sorry he's a bit late,' Bards calls out, opening the driver's door and climbing out to talk to us over the top of the bonnet of his car. 'We had a party at mine last night. It was a good night. You should have been there, Billie! Next time, yeah?' His mouth curves into a thin-lipped smile, his eyes roaming down to my feet and back up again. 'And feel free to wear that little tennis outfit.'

Harley shoots him a warning look, but doesn't say anything. I glower at Bards.

'Whoa!' Bards laughs. 'Sorry, Ice Princess – didn't mean to offend.'

'What the fuck, Harley?' I say, deciding to pretend as though Bards isn't here and ignore him completely. 'You're so late.'

'Oi, who are you – his mother?' Bards snorts, determined to retain control of the situation. 'What's the big deal? He's here, isn't he? Look, off he goes. Fucking pointless. Harley, sack it off, mate, and let's go back to mine.'

Harley is slinking towards the court, opening the gate and wincing as it squeaks.

'What are you playing at, Harley?' Nick says, shaking his head at him.

'Okay, come on, people – I think we can all chill out a bit, yeah?' Bards calls out gruffly before Harley has the chance to answer. 'It's only tennis.' He raps his knuckles impatiently on the bonnet. 'I don't know why he's bothering, to be honest.'

Nick looks fiercely at Bards. 'If you were a true friend, then you would support and encourage his decision to take part in this tournament.'

Bards tips his head back and barks with laughter. 'All right, calm down, mate – you're not in a fucking movie. I don't need a pep talk.'

'Bards,' Harley says in a warning tone, finally finding his voice.

'What?' Bards shrugs. 'Why are you wasting your time with these two, man?'

Harley sighs, rubbing his forehead as he wanders over to us. 'Bards, you should go. I'll catch up with you later.'

Bards sighs. 'Fine. I was just having your back, but whatever.' He starts to climb back into the driver's seat, stopping to peer over the roof of the car at us. 'Let's be real here – you're not actually going to make it to Wimbledon, right? You know that.' He sniggers as he slides into his seat, shutting the driver's door behind him and then winding down the window of the passenger side so he can call out, 'You're fucking kidding yourselves.'

Cackling with laughter, he turns on the engine, music blaring out of the radio, and the spin of his wheels echoes across the court as he drives off out of the car park way too fast.

As silence falls, Nick and I turn to look at Harley.

Harley takes off his sunglasses, pinching the bridge of his nose with his thumb and forefinger. When he opens his eyes, we can see that they're bloodshot.

'Sorry,' he murmurs so quietly, I can barely hear him.

'Yeah, you should be,' Nick says in a voice I haven't heard him use before. It's hard, cold and laced with disappointment.

Harley looks physically pained. 'I got carried away last night. It's hard to say no to Bards. If it helps, I'm paying for it now.'

'It doesn't help. Will it happen again?' Nick demands to know.

Harley shakes his head.

'It had better not. Billie's not the only one in your partnership with something at stake here, remember,' Nick says through gritted teeth. 'Oh, and don't bring your so-called *friend* near my court ever again. Understood?'

Harley nods.

'I'll go and set up for the lesson,' Nick grumbles, before turning to walk to the back of the court, muttering something inaudible under his breath.

'I don't think I've ever seen Nick pissed off before,' I remark.

'That's because he's your coach, not your uncle.'

'Maybe you need to start thinking of him as your coach *rather* than your uncle. Then you'd show up to his lessons on time.'

'I don't need a lecture from you, thanks,' he snaps. 'I said I was sorry.'

'You have no right to get mad at me right now. I *told* you what this means to me.'

'Fucking hell, Billie, just drop it, yeah? I know it might be hard for you to get your head around, but some people have lives outside of the court.'

My jaw tenses. I drop my eyes to the ground.

'What did he mean, I'm not the only one with something at stake here?' I ask.

'Nothing.'

'I thought you were doing this for me as some kind of ... favour.'

'And why would I want to do that?' he mutters crossly. He drops his bag from his shoulder, bending down to unzip it. 'I'm here now, okay? Let's just play tennis.'

*

The ball flies past us, zipping straight down the centre line. When Harley doesn't make the slightest attempt to go for it, I throw my hands up in exasperation.

'What the hell?' I cry out. 'You didn't even try!'

'Are you serious?' He looks at me wide-eyed. 'That should have been yours!'

'I couldn't have got that.'

'Yes, you could. You left it on purpose,' he accuses.

'What does that mean?'

'It means you're trying to make me look bad.'

'Oh grow up, Harley.'

'*You* grow up, Billie. All session you've been waiting for me to fuck up.'

'I haven't done much waiting,' I clap back, moving towards him as he marches at me, ready to face him head on. 'It's been one fuck up after another.'

'Like you've been doing much better.'

'I've been covering for you!' I argue, as we come to an abrupt halt in front of each other. 'You've been moping around, letting me do ninety per cent of the work.'

'Here we go – all hail the great Billie Dawson,' he says, tucking his racket under his arm so his hands are free to clap slowly in my face. 'No one can live up to her standards.'

'It's not my standards you have to live up to, Harley. It's Wimbledon's.'

He rolls his eyes. 'We're not on the grass, yet. This is called practice.'

'I'd call it a fucking disaster.'

'Then maybe we should quit,' he hisses.

'Gladly!'

'Great.'

'*Great*.'

Neither of us budge, our blazing eyes locked, jaws tense, our chests heaving up and down. Whoever flinches first loses.

'Hey! Both of you, calm down,' Nick orders, and I hear his footsteps approach. 'That's enough.' He appears in between us, holding up his hands. 'Clearly, we need a break.'

I snort. 'That's an understatement.'

'Do you even want us to get to the tournament?' Harley asks me, narrowing his eyes. 'Or would you rather we fail just so you get to say you were right about me being a fuck-up?'

'You're doing a great job of proving that without me having to say a thing.'

'Oi!' Nick raises his voice. 'I said, *that's enough*. Both of you.' He shakes his head in disapproval. 'Look, I know it's been a rocky start, but there were moments today that haven't been all that bad. Let's call it there, and come back tomorrow with fresh heads –' he looks pointedly at Harley, who drops his eyes to his feet – 'and open minds.'

That last bit is directed to me. I look away, too.

'Tomorrow, I want to see you *trying* to work together,' Nick continues. 'Your talent and fitness will only get you so far. You need to be a team if you want to win.'

Harley lifts his head to glare at me. 'I'm not the one who didn't get the memo about teamwork, Coach.'

Nick stares him down, reiterating calmly, 'Tomorrow, we try again. Got it?'

With a lacklustre shrug, Harley storms away, swiping his bag up from the side of the court and striding out through the gate. I shake my head at his back as he goes.

'This was never going to work,' I say bitterly.

'Not with your mentality, it won't,' Nick comments.

'*My* mentality?' I turn to him in disbelief. 'He's the one who showed up hungover and late! He's the one who made the mistake!'

'Yeah, and you made sure he didn't forget it.'

I stare at him, my mouth hanging open.

Nick gives me a stern look, refusing to back down. 'How well would you play alongside someone who makes it clear they don't think you're good enough?'

'I ... I would work hard to prove them wrong,' I say haughtily.

'You shouldn't have to feel like you have to prove *anything* to your teammate. They should be the one person who believes in you when no one else does, not even yourself. If you already think you're a loser, you'll probably lose.'

I watch Harley push open the door to the club so hard, it

swings and hits the wall with a resounding thud. I frown, guilt twisting my stomach into an uncomfortable knot. I know how it feels to not be seen as good enough. I've felt that all my life.

'Go home, Billie. I'll see you here tomorrow,' Nick says gently. 'And let's hope Harley comes back, too.'

CHAPTER NINE

Harley and I both show up for training the next day, but apparently we're not on speaking terms. Neither of us have said a word directly to each other all morning.

Actually, that's not entirely true. We did have a brief exchange when we arrived on the court at the same time.

'Hi,' I said.

'Hi,' he replied curtly, eyes averted.

I opened my mouth to say something else, maybe ask how he was, but then bottled it and clamped it shut again. He remained silent, hovering nearby, waiting for Nick to come over to give us instruction. The air between us felt tense and brittle, as though we each had plenty to say, but I'd rather stay silent than fight. Clearly he felt the same.

On the court, we're not speaking, either. We listen to Nick's guidance and follow his instructions: we dutifully hit our groundstrokes; we move in for volleys on cue; we take turns to practise our serves. And neither of us say a damn word the entire time. Nick suggests we round off the end of this gruelling session of repetitive drills with some rallies, noting that next time we'll be trying out various strategies.

'But you've worked hard this morning, so let's just play some tennis,' he concludes.

Harley nods, lifting his T-shirt to wipe the sweat off his brow. My eyes drift to his toned abs on display. Something flutters in my chest. He catches me looking and I turn away, heat rising up my neck and through my face. When he doesn't say anything and walks away to the other end of the court, it somehow makes me feel worse. Before yesterday, Harley would have teased me for glancing his way. That cocky smile of his would have made an appearance and he would have made a joke about me liking what I see, a stupid comment that would have made me roll my eyes and retort that he had a vivid imagination.

I can almost play out the entire exchange of how it would have gone in my head.

He's not playful or teasing today, though. *He hates me.*

Our rallies are solid, but boring, neither of us enjoying it. The only sound coming from our court is the thuds of the ball bouncing on the ground and the ensuing smacks of it hitting our rackets. Every now and then, Nick will throw in a 'nice' or a 'good'.

It's not a bad session. We're not arguing at least. But it's deflated and gloomy. There's no spirit in our performance. No heart. We won't win like this.

Just before Harley leaves, I blurt out, 'I'll see you tomorrow?'

He glances over at me, taking a swig from his water bottle before replacing the cap and saying, 'Yep, see you tomorrow,' his voice emotionless, his expression neutral.

I watch him exit the court, wondering if it would have been better for us to have been arguing all morning. The indifference feels worse.

When the next session starts out much the same, I find my anger towards Harley growing. *How can he bear this?* I think, as Nick knocks a ball to my backhand and I send it clumsily back to him. Nick easily returns my ball to Harley's forehand and he places it beautifully down the line. *Why isn't he saying anything?* One of us has to crack.

'You're distracted, Billie,' Nick accuses, when I send the next ball into the net.

'Sorry, Coach,' I say quietly, looking down at the ground.

I can hear Nick's sigh from over here. Then come his footsteps and he's now our end of the court, gesturing for us both to come towards him.

'Right, you two, I want to try something,' he announces. 'Weapons down.'

Harley and I glance at each other in confusion.

Nick rolls his eyes. 'Rackets on the ground. Come on. Chop-chop.'

Puzzled, I lower my racket carefully onto the court by my feet. Harley does the same.

'You both have beautiful voices,' Nick begins. 'I would like you to use them. But I'd like you to use them for *good*. I would like each of you to tell the other one something you admire about their game.'

I blink at him. 'What?'

'I would like you to tell Harley what you admire about his tennis,' he explains clearly and slowly, before looking to Harley, 'and I would like you to do the same for Billie.'

Harley and I share another bewildered look.

'It's very simple,' Nick presses. 'And we're not going to play any tennis until you have completed this task. So, as you're both grown-ups and I trust you can carry this out without supervision, I'm going to head over there –' he nods to the back of the court – 'and give my husband a call. There's no rush on this. Have a think and then speak up when you have something good to say. No raised voices and no petty criticisms.' He gives both of us a hard stare. 'Do you understand?'

I fold my arms across my chest. 'Fine.'

Harley nods.

'Good,' Nick says brightly, before he walks away.

Harley and I stand in silence.

When I finally sneak a glance at him, I see his forehead is creased in concentration, his eyes fixed to the ground. He doesn't look enthusiastic about this direction from Nick. I exhale in frustration as I look away.

Fuck's sake. This is so stupid.

Both of us are too stubborn to speak first. This is never going to wo—

'You go for every shot.'

I snap my head up at Harley's voice. He's still not looking at me, but I stare at him long enough to meet his gaze when he eventually drags it up. He must read the confusion in my expression because he feels the need to explain his comment.

'I've always admired that about you. The way you go for every shot, even when it doesn't seem possible. You still try. And a lot of the time, you do return it. It's like you won't accept that anything is . . . impossible.'

I don't say anything at first, stunned.

'It makes me want to try harder,' he adds quickly in a quieter voice.

'Oh. Thanks. That's . . .' I trail off.

I've never really thought about that being something I do. I guess now he's said it, I do rarely let a ball fly past me without at least trying for it, even when I think it's out of reach. I didn't think anyone else would notice that about me.

'Thanks,' I repeat.

'It's the truth, so . . .' He shrugs.

I take a deep breath. 'I like your style.'

His eyebrows shoot up in surprise, before he tugs at his

T-shirt. 'Really? I've never been that into fashion, but I have tried harder to make an effort with—'

'Not your clothes, doofus; I meant your style of tennis.'

'Oh!' He breaks into a smile, laughing at himself. 'Okay, that makes more sense.'

I can't help but smile back, amused at his mistake. 'It's kind of effortless the way you play. If we're being completely honest . . .' I breathe out all the air in my cheeks, knowing that I may live to regret this but deciding it's worth the risk if Nick thinks this kind of thing will help. 'I've actually always been a bit jealous of you.'

'You've been jealous of me? *Please* explain.'

'I have to work so hard to be good at this,' I say, gesturing around the tennis court. 'Whereas you look like you're not even breaking a sweat when you play. It's like . . .'

He sees me struggling to describe it and makes a suggestion: 'Raw natural talent?'

'Not exactly how I was going to put it, but, yeah, something like that.'

His eyes light up. 'Dawson, you think I'm a star!'

'Okay, calm down. Now you're running away with it.'

'Basically, I'm a young Federer.'

'God, you're not comparing yourself to *Federer*,' I groan.

'I'm paraphrasing what you said to me. Wow. Do I look taller to you? I feel taller.'

I fight a laugh, but it's unstoppable. Not just because he's being ridiculous, but also because something has cracked between us and he's acting more … himself. I'm laughing with relief at the same time.

'Thanks, Dawson,' he says, his grin widening. 'All this time you've been secretly watching me, studying me, admiring my – how did you put it? Oh yeah – *effortless* style.'

'I've barely noticed you. Coach asked me to come up with a compliment and I'm simply thinking on my feet.'

He waggles his finger at me. 'Oh no, you can't take it back now. You've put it out there into the universe. Fuck. I feel inspired. No, wait, *I've* inspired *you*. And that brings me a lot of joy. You ain't seen nothing yet, though. I'm going to play with so much grace, it's going to blow your mind, Dawson.'

'You're insufferable.'

'All this time I thought I was barely on your radar, but you've been *jealous*. I can't believe this.'

'I can't believe you thought I was talking about your clothes.'

He chuckles. 'Yeah, I'm a bit embarrassed about that actually.'

'You should be.'

'In that case, you should be embarrassed about calling me a doofus,' he retorts smugly, quirking a brow. 'What are you, six years old?'

'Okay, can we get back to playing tennis, please,' I call over to Nick.

'I'd love to,' Harley says, grabbing his racket before he backs away from me, spinning it up in the air and catching it. He points it at me. 'Get ready for some envy-inducing talent coming your way.'

I roll my eyes.

'How did that go?' Nick says, sauntering back to me while Harley swings his racket through the air, making his own *swish* sound effects with his mouth.

I sigh. 'The good news is, we're speaking again, and—'

'Come on, Dawson – I want to inspire you,' Harley calls out, before pretending to smash an imaginary ball and going, '*Bam!*' He winks at me. 'Effortless. Am I right?'

'And the bad news is, we're speaking again,' I murmur, picking up my racket and reluctantly moving to join Harley at the baseline, ignoring the satisfied smirk on Nick's face.

CHAPTER TEN

Melrose's finest 🌿🖤

> **Billie**
> Important question

> **Jess**
> Go

> **Billie**
> What food do you want tonight?

> **Jess**
> What kind of question is that?
> It's movie night
> We ALWAYS have pizza on movie night

Billie
Ok phew
I was just checking
Last time Kat said we could think about shaking it up
She suggested sushi

Jess
SUSHI?!?!
No
I love sushi
But movies and … SUSHI?!
That is not a thing
Kat, explain yourself
…

Kat, you've left this question unanswered all day

Billie
She's leaving us hanging
Building suspense

Jess
Are you upset about the sushi thing, Kat?
If you really want sushi, we can do sushi
…

Kat, are you okay?
You haven't checked your phone in hours

Kat
Hey! Sorry, am with Bards
How would you feel about going out tonight?

Jess
I thought the plan was a movie night?

Billie
Yeah, we've talked about a movie night all week

Jess
I want to have a proper catch-up
Bills has been training hard and we've been out a lot
Also I'm already in my PJs

Kat
You could get out of your PJs ...

Jess
I thought you were really up for movie and pizza!

> You were saying how much you've been going out recently and how you wanted a night in with the girls???

> **Kat**
> I know, but Bards thought it might be fun to hang out again tonight

> **Jess**
> Oh ok

> **Billie**
> You go out tonight with Bards if you like!
> We can do movie night another time

> **Jess**
> Yeah go for it
> I think I'm going to have a night in though

> **Kat**
> Don't you think it would be fun to have a big night out together?
> The three of us!

Jess
Wouldn't Bards be there, too?

Kat
Yeah, but a few of his mates are going
He can hang with them and I can hang with you!

Jess
I've been out a lot with you and Bards recently
It's been a lot of fun, but think I'll have a chilled one
Bills, OK if I come to yours still?

Billie
Yes please!!
Tom's ordering the pizza now

Kat
Ok
Make sure he orders enough for me too

Jess
Wait, you're not going out with Bards then?

> **Kat**
> And let you two have all the fun without me?
> No way

> **Billie**
> YAY!!

> **Kat**
> I'll be a bit late, will leave Bards's in a bit
> Then have to go home to get my PJs
> Don't eat all the pizza before I get there

> **Jess**
> I can make no promises

'I don't get it, Billie,' Tom says, carefully placing Claude on his shoulder before nestling back into the cushion of the sofa. 'I thought you and Harley were on good terms.'

'We are. Sort of.' I sit cross-legged on the floor, picking up a slice of pizza.

'They're speaking, but they're not *communicating*,' Jess informs Tom in an overly dramatic voice, mimicking what I told her earlier. Curled up on the chair by the window, a pizza box resting on the arm, she flashes a mischievous grin at me. 'Apparently, that's supposed to make sense.'

'Oh, *I'm* communicating with Harley,' I correct Jess loftily. 'He's just not listening.'

'So, basically, you're telling him what to do all the time and not letting him have any say in it,' Tom assumes, sharing a conspiratorial smile with Jess that I don't much care for. 'I take it he's not a pushover like me, then.'

'You're not a pushover!'

'I did always let you direct me on the court,' he reasons, admiring Claude as he makes his way down Tom's arm. 'Mostly because you had the best strategies and tactics. But maybe Harley has his own ideas he wants to try out. He is a different player to me – our usual strategies might not sit so well with him. Have you tried listening to *his* suggestions?'

'His suggestions are stupid.'

'Very mature,' Tom says sarcastically as Jess giggles.

He may be annoying, but one of the best things about having a movie night tonight is that Tom has been able to join us. He's had a tough few days, but he's really perked up with the company. He got his blood test results back – it wasn't just a sore throat. Turns out he has a really bad case of glandular fever that was on the brink of developing into something much worse since he'd ignored all the symptoms so long. When we found out, I teased him about who he's been secretly hooking up with, since it's commonly spread through kissing. He said there were a few candidates, admitting to having had a *lot* of fun at all the parties he'd gone to after finishing A-Levels.

As soon as I asked, I regretted it. Gross.

'Have you told Harley to play topless yet? I really think that could be the answer to your problems,' Kat adds, busy messaging someone on her phone – probably Bards.

She always seems to be messaging him when she's not with him. When Jess pulled her up on it, she explained that he gets upset if she doesn't reply straight away.

'Thanks for the input, Kat,' I say drily.

'Any time, babe.'

'What are you doing ogling other guys? I thought you had a *boyfriend*,' Jess teases.

'I'm allowed to window-shop,' Kat says, before wrinkling her nose. 'Although, don't tell Bards that. He's got a very sexy jealous streak.'

'Are you sure it's sexy?' Jess checks.

'A little bit of possessiveness isn't a bad thing,' Kat contends.

'Hang on, you didn't correct Jess when she referred to Bards as your *boyfriend*,' I point out, my eyes widening at her. 'Are you two official?'

'Yes, we are, and before you say anything, I know it's fast,' she announces, lifting her chin. 'But when you know, you know. I like that he's so open about his feelings.'

'Wait, you're ... serious? You're already exclusive?' Tom gapes at her. 'You hardly know this guy!'

Kat shrugs. 'I know enough about him to know it's the real deal. It's amazing. We want to be around each other all the time.'

'Is it *healthy* to be together all the time, though, when you're still getting to know him?' Jess asks, her eyebrows raised as Tom shakes his head, bewildered. 'I would find it a bit ... suffocating.'

'It's nice to feel wanted,' Kat tells her. 'I'm used to staring at my phone waiting for a message that's never coming. I hate guys who play games.' She hesitates as her phone vibrates for the third time in two minutes. 'He does check in quite a bit, but he's thinking of me. It's sweet.'

'Didn't you say when you got here that he'd had a go at you for choosing to spend tonight with us instead of going out with him?' Jess notes.

'Yeah, and I told him off for being an arsehole,' Kat says sternly. 'Don't worry, I can hold my ground. Why do you think he's messaging so much now? He feels bad about earlier.' Her eyes mist over into a dreamy daze as she reads a new message on her screen. 'He says he's going to make it up to me with a date tomorrow.'

A flash of concern crosses Jess's expression, too fast for Kat to notice, but I recognize it. It instantly puts me on edge. Where I'm guarded and blunt, often too quick to brush someone aside, Jess will always look for the good in everyone, playing to their strengths so they show their best side. If Jess is unsure about Bards, it's not a good sign.

'You know I've always liked a bad boy,' Kat continues with a wistful sigh. 'Bards is, like, the full package. He's ready to commit, *but* he has an edge. It's perfect. The dream combination. He's a bad boy who texts back.'

'So, what you're saying is, he's sweetly dangerous,' Jess sums up.

'Exactly,' Kat declares proudly. 'And have you *seen* his body?'

'If you start banging on about his biceps again, I'm going to leave the room,' Jess threatens, lifting her eyes to the ceiling.

'I like a man who can throw me around,' Kat continues, ignoring her.

'Okay, too much information,' Tom mutters.

'Oh! Jess got a girl's number a couple of nights ago, did she tell you?' Kat says, sitting up excitedly.

I turn to Jess to look at her accusingly. 'No!'

'Because there's nothing to tell,' she claims, pinching a mushroom between her fingers and peeling it off her slice, dropping it back into the box. 'I got her number, but nothing's happened. She didn't do it for me. We didn't have much to talk about. She was gorgeous, but there was no spark.'

'Conversation is important,' Tom agrees, his eyes flickering to Kat as he balances Claude in the palm of his hand. 'If you want a proper connection. It's not just about . . . muscle.'

Jess and I catch each other's eye. She suppresses a smile.

'I don't think muscle is top of Jess's list, Tom,' Kat says, giving him a strange look, completely oblivious to any undertone, before turning back to Jess. 'But it's a shame it didn't come to anything. I was excited for you.'

'Hey, it was still fun to flirt with someone,' Jess says, her eyes twinkling at us. 'Good practice before I start uni in Manchester.'

'Oh my god, I cannot *wait* to visit once I'm back from Europe,' Kat squeals, clapping her hands. 'Such a cool city with the best nightlife!'

'And a much better gay scene than here in Berkshire, that's for sure.' Jess laughs. 'So I wouldn't worry about my love life, Kat.'

'You're not the one I worry about,' she responds, her gaze shifting pointedly to me.

'Hey!' I say defensively as Jess cackles with laughter.

'What, it's fair – right, Jess?' Kat says, grinning. 'You never allow yourself some fun.'

'Bloody hell, not you, too,' I groan, running a hand through my hair. When I notice them all looking at me in confusion, I add bitterly, 'Harley mentioned it.'

Jess squints at me curiously. 'He was interested in your love life?'

I narrow my eyes at her. '*No*. He ... made an unwelcome and intrusive comment about how I haven't really ... *been* with anyone since Caleb. Not that it's his business. Or anyone else's, thanks very much.'

'Please, we're your best friends – of course it's our business,' Kat argues.

'I'm happy for it to be absolutely none of my business,' Tom mumbles, but he's swiftly ignored.

'It's not like you don't have people falling over themselves to catch your attention,' Kat tells me, her eyes glinting. 'Bards told me that loads of his mates talk about you.'

'I think he may have been saying that to win you over,' I inform her, unimpressed. 'He called me "Ice Princess" the other day.'

'Were you being warm and sweet to him?' she asks with a knowing smile.

I hesitate, grimacing. 'I was maybe a tiny bit . . . frosty.'

'You? Being cold to a guy? Outrageous,' Tom says with dramatic zeal.

I glare at him.

'You want my opinion, Bills? I think if you wanted Harley Pierce, you could have him,' Kat says pompously. 'All that time you're spending together training, running around the court, sweating, panting—'

I burst out laughing. 'You are making it sound a lot sexier than it is, trust me.'

'Personally, I don't know what you're waiting for. You never know,' she says, wiggling her eyebrows at me, 'a little passion *off* the court might help things *on* the court.'

'Eugh,' Tom utters quietly in disgust.

'Okay, Harley is my tennis partner, nothing more,' I say defensively, before taking a bite of pizza. 'I don't ... I don't look at him that way.'

'*Everyone* looks at him that way,' Kat claims. 'Except Jess, for obvious reasons.'

'I can still appreciate his beauty,' Jess claims. 'And humour.' I shoot her a look of betrayal, but she shrugs in response. 'What? He's funny.'

'He's arrogant, childish and self-centred,' I list.

'How is he self-centred when he's going out of his way to help you?' Tom points out. 'He didn't have to partner up with you and spend his summer training.'

'I don't know,' I say, wiping my hands with a napkin as I recall what Nick said about something being at stake for Harley, too. 'I think he might need this. No idea why, though.'

'Well, I think he's fun,' Kat declares, before grinning wickedly at me. 'And as long as he's not self-centred in bed, then why should you care?'

'You know, you're rapidly turning into one of those annoying, smug people because you're having great sex,' Jess tells her bluntly.

'Yes, I am, and I want my best friends to be smug about having great sex, too,' Kat counters.

'No chat about my sister's sex life while I'm in the room,' Tom says, wrinkling his nose as Kat giggles away to herself.

'There's no sex life to chat about,' I assure him. 'Like I say, Harley and I are doubles partners. We're barely friends.'

'Maybe that's your problem,' Tom comments, gently stroking Claude's little head with his forefinger.

I frown at him. 'What do you mean?'

'That could be why you're not playing your best together,' he says, distracted by Claude. 'Think about it: why do me and you play well as a team? We trust each other. We have each other's backs.' He tears his eyes away from the gecko to fix me with a look. 'You have to trust Harley, and he's going to need to trust you. Otherwise, you don't have a chance.'

CHAPTER ELEVEN

The next day, I walk down the path to the end of our fence, round the corner of it and back up the path to Harley's house. I stop in front of his door.

It's taken me all morning to gather the courage to do this. I went on a run first thing and then, after breakfast and a smoothie, I took myself to the courts for an hour or so to practise my serves and groundstroke placement and precision. I showered, got dressed in a T-shirt and high-waisted denim shorts, came home and lurked around my bedroom for a bit, glancing through the window every now and then over at his house, practising what I would say. I put on make-up, brushed my hair, and then took a deep breath before marching down the stairs.

'Where are you going?' Tom called out as I passed his open door.

'To build some trust,' I admitted reluctantly.

Now, I'm here, and all I have to do is knock on the door.

I can hear music blaring from inside the house, but it's not Harley's. I know that because he doesn't really listen to music, or if he does, then he must use headphones. I never hear any coming from his room anyway. But his mum likes to blast out music, sometimes late into the night, sometimes singing along to it. She's sort of in key, so it's not too bad, but more often than not, the words are slurred.

His dad's car isn't in the driveway, so I'm going to go ahead and guess that the current song by the Rolling Stones blasting out from the kitchen is his mum's choice.

Reaching up, I rap my knuckles on the door.

At first, nothing happens. They probably didn't hear it over the music, so I knock again, but louder this time. The music doesn't get turned down or shut off, but I hear a woman's voice screech over it, '*Harley!* Get the door, will you? I'm busy getting in character!'

I step back, hearing the repetitive thud of footsteps descending the stairs. The door swings open and Harley is there in faded jeans and a T-shirt, clearly startled to find me on his doorstep.

'Hey,' I say awkwardly.

'Dawson,' he says, holding the door open with his foot as he folds his arms to take me in properly, 'what are you doing here? Did I miss a training session?'

'No, I ... uh ... actually, I wondered if I could come in.'

He stares at me.

'I wanted to talk,' I add stupidly, as if I might be there for anything else.

'Okay,' he says slowly, before standing aside.

I step past him gingerly, my thumbs hooked in the back pockets of my shorts. He closes the door behind me. I've never been in his house before. I stand awkwardly in the hallway, glancing at the framed newspaper cutting on the wall of a theatre review with the headline: Ronnie Pierce Shines in Her West End Debut.

Harley follows my eyeline and sighs.

Jerking his head at it, he says, 'From when we lived in London.'

'Your mum was on the West End?' I say, impressed. 'That's amazing.'

'Yeah, but then my grandparents passed away, left Dad this house, and so we upped sticks from the lights of the big city, moved here and ruined Mum's life,' Harley reels off wearily. 'I'm sure you've heard the story.'

'Actually ... no.'

'Strange, she likes to tell anyone who will listen long enough.' He winces as the volume of the music is turned up and gestures to the stairs. 'Let's go talk in my room.'

'Okay. Should I ... uh ...' I peer down the hallway to the kitchen where I see Ronnie dancing around the table in skinny black jeans and a red off-the-shoulder top, a script in one hand, a glass of wine in the other. 'Should I say hi to your mum?'

'I wouldn't bother,' he says, beginning to climb the stairs. 'Nice of you to be so polite, but she wouldn't appreciate the interruption. She's rehearsing for an audition.'

Tearing my eyes away from her as she sways side to side with her eyes closed, flicking her curly brown hair over her shoulder, I follow him up the stairs, crossing the landing into his room, where he shuts the door firmly behind us.

It's so *neat* in here. The bed is made, his desk is ordered with his laptop front and centre, headphones next to it, and on his bedside table by the lamp is a stack of three books, the top one of which is a Stephen King. A huge map of America covers almost an entire wall of his room with little red pins dotted around it. It smells so good in here, fresh laundry mixed with a hint of his cologne hanging in the air.

'I would offer you a tea or coffee or something, but we should wait until Mum's finished her … rehearsal, if that's okay,' he begins, hovering by the door as he watches me wander into the centre of the room.

'No, it's fine,' I say quickly, spinning round to face him. 'What's the audition for?'

'A new play by an upcoming British writer,' he says with a shrug. 'They're putting it on at the local theatre with a hope it will tour. The role she's going for is the long-suffering girlfriend of a washed-up rockstar.' He offers a wry smile. 'Apparently, she's perfect for it.'

'I hope she gets it.'

'Me too. It's never fun when she doesn't.' He presses his lips together. 'So, what did you want to talk about?'

'Oh. Right. I . . . I wanted to . . . apologize.'

The corners of his mouth curve up.

Fuck's sake, I knew he'd be like this.

'You want to apologize to me,' he repeats, as though to check he's not hearing things.

'Yes,' I say in all seriousness. 'I think we need to start afresh.'

He quirks a brow. 'Really.'

'I think I may have been a bit unfair on you recently. I haven't been very enthusiastic or welcoming. And I'm sorry for that.'

'Whoa.' His eyes spark with delight. 'Billie Dawson is really apologizing to me. Do you mind if I get out my phone and film this? Just so I can make sure that I'm not making this up when I think about it later. If you could repeat everything you—'

'Harley,' I say sharply, shutting him up, 'it would be helpful if you could be serious. I'm trying to talk to you properly and it doesn't help if you're making fun of me.'

He nods, his expression softening. 'Okay, sorry. You're right. Go ahead.'

'I know our training for the tournament didn't get off to a good start.' I shoot him a hard stare. 'You shouldn't have been late and hungover, but –' I exhale and drop my eyes to the floor – 'I also shouldn't have gone out of my way to make you feel guilty about it. I should have been more friendly and encouraging. I should have been better.'

With trepidation, I return my gaze to Harley.

There's a beat of silence. He's watching me curiously, his intense gaze causing my cheeks to flush with heat.

'If we don't put our all into the practice,' I continue, trying my best to sound calm and collected rather than flustered, 'then it's not just our time we're wasting; it's Nick's, too. I thought if we're going to do this, then we should work on our issues and come back to the court with a brand-new mindset. What do you think?'

'I think that all makes sense.'

I release an inward sigh of relief.

'Good. That's why I wanted to start again. So, yeah. I appreciate that you're going out of your way to help me, and I'm sorry I've been . . . mean.'

He laughs lightly. 'You weren't mean, Dawson.'

'I have been a bit mean.'

'Me too. We pushed each other's buttons.'

'Still, it's up to me to create the right energy and vibe.'

'Dawson, you're not the *captain* of our team,' he teases. 'It's up to both of us to come to the court with the right attitude, and I gave as good as I got. But, look, I appreciate the apology. Can I ask what spurred it on now, though?'

'I've realized that, although I'm glad we're not arguing as much when we play—'

'I wouldn't call it arguing,' he cuts in, stroking his chin thoughtfully. 'More *debating*.'

'Whatever you call it, it's not good for morale when it happens,' I say firmly. 'But that aside, we're also not –' I search for the right word – 'meshing well.'

'You mean, you're ignoring everything I say.'

'And you're ignoring everything *I* say.'

'Okay, we've both proven we're stubborn arseholes. So, how do we solve this conundrum?'

'I thought we would probably listen to each other better if we *knew* each other a bit better. I want to trust you, Harley; I just don't know you well enough.'

He takes a step towards me before bringing his eyes up to meet mine, a bemused smile playing on his lips. 'Dawson,' he says in a low growl, 'are you saying you want to get to know me?'

'Yeah, I *literally* said that,' I say, rolling my eyes. 'Don't make it weird.'

'It's not weird. It's amazing.'

'You're already making it weird.'

'Okay, I hear what you're saying and I think you're onto something. So here's my answer: Yes, I will go on a date with you.'

I wrinkle my nose. 'What? That is *not* what I was saying!'

'How else do you propose we get to know each other?'

'I don't know,' I say, exasperated, glancing around for inspiration. 'We ... hang out.'

'Hang out, maybe get some food, a drink or two ...'

He trails off, his sparkling eyes boring into me.

'Christ, make those *strong* drinks, please, if you're going to act like this,' I mutter, folding my arms across my chest. 'Look, do you want to do this or not? Because I think our game will improve if we know what makes each other tick, but if you're going to be weird about it, then we should just leave things to play out on the court.'

He sighs. 'Worth a try. Fine. A ... *non*-date it is. Hang out, have a couple of drinks, get to know each other and come to respect one another. Maybe even like each other. All in the name of tennis. I'm in if you are.' Harley holds out his hand.

'A non-date,' I repeat, smiling and grasping his hand to shake it. 'I'm in.'

CHAPTER TWELVE

Melrose's finest 🌿❤️

Kat
So ... what are you wearing?

> **Billie**
> Um
> Did you mean to send this message to us?

Jess
Gross, was this for Bards?

Kat
No!
It's for Billie!
I'm asking what you're wearing on your date tonight

Billie
It is NOT a date
I told you
It's a non-date

Kat
Uh-huh
Sure
Whatever the fuck that is

Jess
It's a date

Kat
I shall ask you once again ...
What are you wearing for your date?

Billie
For my NON-DATE
I am wearing a white T-shirt
Black miniskirt with tights
And a blazer
Do you think that's ok?

Jess
Why would you ask us that if it's not a date?

Kat
AHA!
Good point, Jess
So handy having a clever friend

Jess
Glad to be of assistance

Billie
Fine
I don't care what you think
BUT if I did care what you think
What would you say?

Kat
PERFECT
Relaxed but sexy
Great for a first date

Billie
NOT A FIRST DATE

Jess
Where are you going?

Billie
Not sure
He's picked a bar somewhere

Jess
Interesting
He's taking the lead

Billie
So?

Kat
He wants to impress you

Billie
I'm telling you, this is not a date

Jess
That depends

Billie
ON WHAT?!

> **Jess**
> On where he takes you

> **Billie**
> You two are very annoying

> **Kat**
> But you love us so much anyway
> Tell us how it goes!

When Harley messages me to say he's waiting outside, I check my reflection in the mirror one last time. Tom appears in my doorway, giving a low whistle.

'You look nice,' he remarks. 'Not surprising, considering you've taken five hours to get ready.'

I scowl at him. 'More like twenty minutes.'

Both of us are off. It's actually taken me about an hour, which I am fully aware is not the amount of time I should be spending getting ready for a non-date. But once I decided on my outfit, I actually really enjoyed taking my time with my make-up and curling my hair into soft, gentle waves, before deciding what jewellery to wear and which bag to bring. As I spritzed perfumed on my wrists and neck, butterflies dancing around my stomach, I realized that I've been so focused on sport recently, I've missed the fun of getting ready to go out, not knowing what the night might bring.

'I'm serious, you look good. Hey –' he leans an elbow on the doorframe – 'do you think now is a good time to ask Dad if it's all right for me to get a dog? He's being so nice to me because I'm ill. I feel like I should take advantage of his goodwill.'

Turning away from the mirror, I grab my phone and keys, shoving them into my bag. 'Tom, we've been over this. You're going to university; you can't get a dog now.'

'I'd bring the dog with me,' he explains, as I slide past him and head down the stairs.

'Not many halls will let you keep a dog, Tom,' I call back over my shoulder.

'You're so pessimistic.'

'I'm realistic.'

'Same thing,' he huffs, traipsing down the steps after me and leaning on the banister. 'I'll ask Nikesh what he thinks. He's coming over in a minute.'

I sigh, tilting my head at him as I reach for the doorknob. 'Eighteen years old and still having friends over to play PlayStation all night. You're so cool, Tom.'

'Says the girl going on a *friends* date with her too-cool-for-school next-door neighbour.' He gives me a thumbs-up. 'Good one.'

Rolling my eyes, I open the door. 'Don't wait up, nerd.'

'Make good choices, loser.'

Sharing a smile with him as I glance back, I stroll out the

front door and find Harley waiting on the pavement by our fence. He looks up from his phone at the sound of the door shutting behind me and starts. His eyes widen and his lips part a little before they stretch into a smile. Tucking my hair behind my ear, I look down as I walk towards him, smiling modestly at his reaction. I'm relieved he's made a bit of an effort, too, wearing an open shirt over a white T-shirt and jeans. I don't know why either of us are so impressed by each other's outfits, it's not like we were expecting the other to rock up in tennis kit.

'Hey,' he says as I approach. 'You ... uh, you look really nice.'

'Thanks. You do, too.' I bite my lip. 'So, where are we going?'

He holds up his phone. 'I've ordered an Uber. It's not far, but I wasn't sure what kind of shoes you'd be wearing, and I didn't want to make you do a long walk in heels.' He glances down at my white trainers. 'Guess I didn't have to worry.'

'That's thoughtful of you,' I say, unable to conceal a hint of surprise in my voice.

He picks up on it instantly. 'The non-date is working already. You're realizing that I do have the capacity to think about the needs of others.'

I laugh as the Uber pulls up and Harley steps forward to open the door for me, letting me slide in before he shuts it and walks round to the other side. As I put on my seatbelt, my stomach twists into a knot. I tell myself to relax. It's confusing that the set-up of this evening is making this feel like, well, a real date, but I'm sure once we're at the bar and we're talking, things will feel a lot more casual and chilled.

He gets into the car and I inhale a waft of his cologne that makes my heart rate quicken and a warmth pool in my belly. *Why does he have to smell so good?* Sitting here in the back of the car with him silently as we set off, the air feels charged between us.

Bollocks. We should have gone for coffee.

It really isn't that far to the bar he's chosen, but we're both so quiet, the journey there feels much longer. When I glance over to see him staring out the window, I wonder if he's feeling as awkward as I am. The scenario feels too weirdly intense, and it hasn't even started yet.

'Here we are,' the driver announces brightly, pulling up on a busy street.

Getting out, I wait for Harley to join me on the pavement and then follow him past the buzzing pubs, bars and restaurants to a place away from the crowds. It looks small and dingy from the outside and I'm confused by his choice at first, especially as it's been such a nice day and it's a warm evening, but then we go in and the man who greets us at the door leads us through to the garden at the back.

I gasp when I step out into an elegant outside space with luscious green plants and colourful flowers lining the fencing, a canopy of festoon lights overhead, a bar at one end of the garden and a jazz band playing at the other, with small round tables dotted in between where people are chatting and laughing. It's a beautiful setting with a really nice, relaxed vibe. I've only been here for a few seconds and I already think it might be one of my favourite bars in town.

'What . . . what is this place?' I stammer, as we're led to our table.

'It's new,' Harley tells me, thanking the man holding out drinks menus for us as we sit down. 'Cool, right? They have different music nights on.' He glances over to the band. 'Guess tonight it's a jazz night.' He notices my expression as I stare at them. 'What? What is it? You don't like jazz?'

'No, that's not . . .' I swallow, shrugging off my blazer and hanging it over my chair. Having collected myself, I'm able to answer properly. 'I like jazz.'

His eyes light up. 'Really?'

'Yeah. My mum loved it. She used to play it a lot.'

He smiles sadly at me and I immediately feel guilty for bringing her up.

'So this place is really cool,' I say brightly, hoping I haven't made him feel awkward. 'Such a great choice, Harley. I didn't even know it existed, but it's so pretty, very chilled *and* playing my favourite kind of music.' I beam at him. 'It's amazing.'

'Stroke of luck,' he says, holding up his hands.

'What do you want to drink?'

'I'll get the first round,' he insists, already back on his feet to go and order at the bar. 'I owe you a drink, remember? Gin and tonic?'

'Great, thanks.'

Sitting back in my chair, I take a moment to soak in the atmosphere, listening to the live music. This would definitely have been Mum's kind of place: not too fancy and stiff, but still feels special. I feel a tug at my chest. Moments like this, when I think about her, are always bittersweet. It's hard because I miss her so much, but it also feels important to not lock up her memory in a box in my mind that's never accessed. So I don't push away the thought. I gaze around at all the people smiling and talking with their companions and I allow myself to have a moment thinking, *Mum would have loved it here.*

Harley places my drink down in front of me and takes his seat opposite.

'Thank you.'

'You looked like you were in your own world there,' he remarks, holding up his glass to clink it against mine.

I smile, taking a sip and putting my glass down.

'So,' I begin.

He takes a large gulp and then lowers his glass. 'So.'

'How does this work?'

'How does what work?'

'This.' I gesture between us. 'This non-date date where we

get to know each other. Should I ask a question and then you ask a question?'

There's a beat of silence before he tips his head back and laughs. I know he's laughing at me, so I should be annoyed, but it strikes me how infectious his laugh is – his proper belly laugh – and without meaning to, I'm grinning.

'What?' I ask through chuckles. 'Why is that so funny?'

'Because, Dawson, I knew you were efficient, but fucking hell,' he says, leaning back and looking me up and down, 'I didn't realize you were so organized that you plan out your conversations before you have them!'

'Oh god, okay, when you put it like that, it sounds so stupid,' I admit, burying my face in my hands. 'Argh. Pretend I didn't say that.'

'No way – I think it's great,' he says, picking up his drink and taking a gulp, looking smug as hell. 'I like the idea of sticking to a routine in a conversation – your question, my question, your question, my—' He gasps, sitting up straight, his eyes widening at me. 'I just realized! It's like a tennis match. You plan conversations like you plan rallies!'

I shake my head, giggling. 'That is *not* what I do.'

'Your dedication knows no bounds. You play life like you play the game.'

'Please stop.'

'Is that a question? And if so, does that count as yours? Hang on, I just asked two.'

I reach for my drink and take a large gulp. 'I'm never going to live this down.'

'Probably not, no,' he says, tilting his head at me. 'But for what it's worth, I actually don't think it's a terrible idea.' He leans forward, lowering his voice. 'We are in uncharted waters here on a non-date. Who knows how it's supposed to play out? I think taking it in turns to ask questions is a smart plan. So, the big question: who should serve first?'

'Surely me. It was my idea.'

'Okay, you go.'

I sit back, thinking as he watches me curiously. There's a lot of pressure riding on what I'm about to say. I have the power to set the tone for the evening. It can't be too serious and deep, not this early on, and I don't want it to be about tennis. I don't want him wondering if I ever think of anything else.

In this moment right now, what do I want to know about Harley Pierce.

'Okay, I have it,' I declare.

'Wait.' He swallows down some of his gin and tonic, wincing at the bitter tang, and then gives me a nod. 'Go ahead.'

'My first question for you, Harley, is ...' I pause for dramatic effect. 'What is your shot of choice?'

'*What?*'

'You heard me. What shot would you like?'

He holds my gaze, his eyes twinkling. 'Tequila.'

'Tequila it is,' I say, putting my glass down and getting up to go to the bar.

Biting my lip as I lean on the counter waiting to put in my order, I glance back over my shoulder to find him watching me, a smile of amazement on his face. When I return with the shots, carefully lowering them onto our table, the lime wedges balanced on top, I move to take my seat, lifting my shot glass in the air.

'There. I've learned something important about you,' I say.

'And I've learned something about *you*.'

'How?' I ask, confused. 'That was my question.'

'Yeah, but it wasn't one I thought you'd pick, which goes to show you're full of surprises, Dawson, and you're not to be underestimated.' He picks up his shot glass and taps it against mine. 'Exactly the kind of player you want on your side of the court.'

CHAPTER THIRTEEN

'My turn,' Harley says, once we've washed our shots down with a gulp of our drinks. 'Why do you want to win this mixed doubles at Junior Wimbledon so badly? The way you spoke to me after Nick first suggested we do this – when you told me how much this contest means to you – I knew then that there's something more to it than just . . . winning.'

I wince. 'Any chance you can start with a simpler question? I'll need a couple more drinks to answer that one.'

He holds up his hands. 'Fair enough. Put that question on hold. Hmm.' He takes a moment to think. 'Okay, I'll go with a simple one: what do you do to switch off? When you're not training or working out, how do you relax?'

'Normal things. Watch films, read. I read a lot, actually.'

'Yeah? What stuff do you like?' He gives me a pointed look. 'Please don't say something like "books on tennis strategies".'

'I do like things other than tennis.'

'I guess that's what I'm discovering tonight.'

Smiling at him, I stir the straw around my glass. 'I read a lot of fantasy.'

'That's cool. You like escaping to magical worlds.'

'Seems better than the real one sometimes.'

'That, I totally get.'

'You're into horror books, right?' When he looks surprised, I feel the need to add, 'I saw the Stephen King by your bed.'

'Oh right, yeah,' he says. 'Actually, someone recommended I try his books, which I am enjoying, but I'm more into crime thrillers. You know, the real page-turners that have you guessing the whole way through with a big twist at the end.'

'I like those.'

'Those are the sorts of books where you can really shut out the real world. The ones where you're so focused on trying to work out the mystery that you forget what's going on in your life,' he tells me, finishing off the last of his drink. 'But I thought I'd try something new, and so far, King's *The Dark Tower* series is really good. Have you read it?'

I shake my head.

'You might like it. It's fantasy, you know – dark fantasy – as well as horror.'

'I'll add it to my list,' I say eagerly, getting out my phone and opening my notes app.

'Wait, you actually *have* a list?' he asks, aghast. 'When most people say they'll "add it to the list", they don't actually then . . . add it to a list.'

'How do they remember the recommendations?' I muse, typing in *The Dark Tower* series. 'I don't want to forget this one.'

When I finish typing and put my phone back, I find him watching me.

'What? Was that a really dorky thing to do or something?' I ask, laughing at myself.

'No, no, it was nice.' His lips curve into a smile. 'For someone to take something I'm saying seriously. It doesn't happen a lot. I've recommended so many books and films to Bards and I don't think he's ever read or watched one of them. I'll have to be more careful with what I say to you in the future and make sure I don't give you any duds.'

I pick up my glass and take a sip. 'Bards and Kat seem very ... together. An official couple.'

He shifts in his seat. 'Bet you're not too happy about that.'

'I don't know Bards very well and I don't want to judge him from that morning at the courts.' I bring my eyes up to meet his, giving a small smile. 'I've already made that mistake with you.'

'Glad I'm on track to change your mind.' He clears this throat. 'But, hey, I know what Bards is like and how he can come across. We're ... different, but we've been friends a long time. You haven't seen him at his best. He can take things too far and he says some stupid stuff – he's an idiot, but he's a decent guy.'

'As long as he treats Kat well, I'm good. How long have you guys been friends?'

'He was one of my first mates at Burton Grammar,' he tells me, tapping his fingers on the table. 'I was finding it difficult to fit in and was getting in a lot of trouble. I was on my last chance when a teacher busted into the changing rooms where I'd been smoking out the window. He smelt the cigarette and demanded to know who it was – Bards happened to be in there at the same time and took the heat.'

'He said it was him?'

'And got suspended so I wouldn't be expelled.' Harley sighs, rubbing the back of his neck. 'See? A decent guy. I've always felt indebted to him, really,' he adds quietly, before sitting up straight. 'Right, I'll get the next round of drinks in and you can have time to think of your next question for me.'

I don't need time to think about my next question; I've been wondering about it ever since I wandered into his room yesterday.

'Why do you have a map of America on your wall with all those pins in it?' I ask as he returns with the drinks and takes his seat.

'My great escape.' He grins, his eyes lighting up at the chance to talk about it. 'I'm taking a year out before university and I'm going to go travelling in America. I'm going to save up the money, buy a plane ticket, hire a car out there and drive from one place to the next. No exact route, no solid plans, just ... see where the road takes me.'

'Wow. Very Jack Kerouac of you.'

'Isn't it. The adventure of a lifetime. I can't wait.' He gives me a sly smile. 'Bet it makes you nervous that I'm not planning a thorough itinerary.'

'Actually, I think it's cool. Kat is going travelling, too. I'm jealous of these big travel plans. I never even considered the idea,' I admit.

'Maybe you should.' He tilts his head at me. 'Where's Kat going?'

'Interrailing across Europe. She's always wanted to do it. For as long as we've been friends, she's talked about it: all the places she wants to go, the things she wants to see, the people she wants to meet along the way.'

'Sounds like Kat has got a fun summer ahead of her.'

'She does.' I take a sip of my drink, noting him observing me, before placing my glass down slowly. 'I know what you're thinking, Harley.'

'What am I thinking, Dawson?'

'That I'm wasting my – what did you call it? – "Summer of Freedom" by not having any fun plans or travel adventures.'

'That's not what I'm thinking,' he assures me. 'I've always liked your drive.'

I snort. 'Come on.'

'I'm being serious!' he insists, leaning forward on the

table as if to emphasize his point. 'I've been jealous of how motivated you are about everything. You know that speech you gave me in the club, when you were saying how I'd better bring everything to this training and not let you down? I was seriously impressed.'

'No, you weren't!' I laugh. 'You thought I was a control freak.'

'I thought you were *brave*,' he says in such a serious, sincere way, my giggling peters out and I stare at him in surprise. 'You have no idea how lucky you are to feel that ... purpose. To feel so passionate and dedicated that no one is going to stop you. The way you go after what you want, no matter what people think – I envy that.'

I swallow the lump in my throat.

'I do care what people think,' I admit quietly. 'That's why I want this Wimbledon win so badly.' He waits patiently as I pick up my drink to take two large gulps. 'In answer to your earlier question about why I feel like this tournament is everything to me – it's because this is the first time I've ever felt like I might be good enough to win, and I have to win to make up for the time ... the time I lost there.'

His frown deepens, his mouth a straight, hard line as he hangs on my every word.

'When Tom won the Fourteen and Under Boys' Tournament at Wimbledon, I lost it – the girls' tournament, I mean,' I explain, tucking my hair behind my ear. 'It doesn't sound like a big deal, and I guess it's not really to most people, but it meant a lot to me because that was the last match my mum ever saw me play. And I lost.'

Harley's lips part and his eyes widen, glistening with sympathy. I keep going, hurrying to get the words out before I can't.

'Since then, Dad's made it obvious that he doesn't think I'm good enough at anything,' I say, my voice a little hoarse now. I drop my eyes to my drink on the table, running a finger down the condensation on my glass. 'Tom's the winner and I'm the loser. The disappointment, never meeting expectations. The curse of being a twin, I guess. The constant comparison. Anyway, my plan is to change everything by winning this summer.'

I quickly pick up my drink to take a swig, unable to bring myself to look at him.

'I'm sorry about your mum, Billie.'

'Thanks,' I say with a wave of my hand. 'It was a long time ago.' I lift my eyes to meet his.

'I know, but ...' He takes a deep breath, looking troubled. 'Still. I'm sorry.'

I nod, offering him a grateful smile. 'Thank you. Okay, so –' I roll back my shoulders, brightening my tone to lift the mood – 'my turn to ask you a question.'

'I believe you're jumping the gun there. The last official question of our game was you asking me about the map on my wall.'

'But then I answered your official question from earlier about why the junior tournament was so important to me. So, *technically*, the spotlight swings back to you now.'

He chuckles, admitting defeat. 'Fine, I'll let you have it.'

Leaning forward, I rest my elbows on the table, looking him right in the eye. 'This tournament – what's in it for you?'

'What makes you think there's anything in it for me but the pleasure of your company and a shot at the big time?'

I roll my eyes. 'You're a charming guy, Harley, but I don't believe you're offering up part of your "Summer of Freedom" to help me out of the goodness of your heart. Nick said there was something at stake for you here – what is it? Why are you doing this?'

Harley sits back, unfazed by my interrogation-style questioning. 'America.'

I frown at him. 'America? But Wimbledon is—'

'Please don't feel the need to explain where Wimbledon is to me,' he cuts in, rolling his eyes. 'The Wimbledon tournament will contribute to my America plans. Financially.'

'Juniors don't win any money.'

'I'm well aware. But Nick has offered to match whatever I earn this summer – you know he's my godfather?'

'I didn't. He's your mum's brother, right?'

He nods. 'And more of a father figure than my dad. I'm lucky to have him in my life, otherwise ... let's just say he's the only one who's offered me a bit of direction.'

'And he's going to help pay for your travels.'

'That's right,' he says, his chest heaving up with a deep breath in. 'But on the condition that I work hard, prove I have some kind of motivation in life, don't get in any trouble – basically, not be an arsehole and prove to him I'm worthy of his hard-earned cash. It's seriously generous of him and I know better than to fuck up. When this opportunity came up, Nick explained that it would be a good chance for me to show him what I'm made of. If I help you on your journey to Wimbledon, I'm one step closer to my journey out of here.'

'Wow. Nick sounds like a really great uncle.'

'Like I said, I'm lucky to have him.' Harley takes a sip of his drink, his brow furrowing. 'My dad's not around much. Less and less these days, to be honest, and that's probably a good thing. I think he's met someone else. Someone at work.'

'Oh. I'm ... sorry.'

Harley shrugs. 'It is what it is. He's a coward. The problem is, we need him. It's not like Mum's raking in the money with all these auditions that don't usually turn into anything. I love her, but she's not very reliable. And she doesn't think I'll amount to anything.'

'I'm sure that's not—'

'It's true,' he interjects, fixing me with a stare. 'Look, Billie, I imagine it's difficult feeling like you haven't met your parents' expectations, but at least someone had some for you in the first place.' He drops his eyes to his lap. 'It's hard to believe in yourself when no one else does. But hey –' he looks up, attempting a weak smile – 'maybe I get to change things, too, this summer. With this tournament, I get to pretend I'm going somewhere in life, act as though I'm motivated enough. Fake it till you make it, right?'

I feel a rush of sadness that's swiftly replaced by a fierce determination.

'Maybe this is your chance to prove them all wrong – you don't necessarily need to fake anything,' I say sternly. 'I can help you find motivation, don't worry about that. And if you really want to win, well, I believe you can.'

He breaks into a wide grin. 'You think so, Dawson?'

'Yes, I do. You've got that *raw natural talent*, remember?' I say drily. 'If you decide that you want to win this thing, you could be a serious threat.'

He watches me, his eyes glinting from the canopy of lights overhead. 'Especially when I'm playing alongside you.'

'Exactly. We've got this.'

A few seconds pass as we hold each other's gaze.

Eventually, he sucks in a breath and rubs his hands together.

'Right. More shots?' he suggests.

'Yeah,' I say before I can think too much about it. 'More shots.'

CHAPTER FOURTEEN

As soon as I wake up the next day, I know what I have to do. The non-date last night turned out to be a fun evening, and despite the headache, I don't regret a moment of it. I'm starting to learn that I may have been wrong about Harley Pierce, and that, with a bit of a nudge, he might be wrong about himself.

Which is why I'm standing outside his house in my gym kit, throwing pebbles at his bedroom window. He's not picking up his phone or answering his messages, so I've been reduced to old-school methods of getting his attention.

The first two pebbles knocking against his window pane go unanswered, but the third gets the reaction I'm after. His face appears at the window and I hear him groan before he begrudgingly opens it, peering down at me. He's topless and his hair is dishevelled in that sexy just-woken-up way. I push aside the unwelcome and *deeply unprofessional* thoughts of how it would feel to run my fingers through it, and beam up at him.

'Good morning!' I say chirpily, dropping the rest of the pebbles and wiping the dirt off my hands.

'What the hell are you doing?' comes the grumpy reply, but I will not be deterred.

'We're going running!'

'The fuck we are.'

'Time to get dressed – let's go,' I encourage, waving for him to come join me.

'Dawson, in case your memory is as hazy as mine, we had some drinks last night,' he says, squinting down at me, his voice hoarse. 'What is wrong with you? *No one* is up this early.'

'Winners are,' I say, fully aware that I sound like a twat but leaning into it. 'And you, my friend, are a winner.'

'You're a fucking robot. How are you this . . . *perky*?'

'I'm excited to go for a run with you! What better way to get rid of a hangover than sweat it out?'

'That's literally the worst thing you can do for a hangover,' he grumbles, rubbing his forehead. 'You need to rehydrate, not do anything that makes you even more dehydrated.'

'Look at you speaking sense this early!' I say brightly through a wide grin. 'You're proving that you are definitely able to get up and come for a workout.'

He heaves a sigh, resting his head in his hands as he leans against his windowsill. 'You have a problem, Dawson.'

'I know. I'm looking at him.'

'Very funny,' he mutters, lifting his head to narrow his eyes at me.

'Come on, Harley, you said you needed real motivation,' I point out, putting my hands on my hips. 'I'm here to help you find it. Let's do this properly. What's the point in taking part if you're not going to try to win? Let's put in the work as a *team*.'

'Oh god, you're giving me a Disney-sports-movie pep talk and the sun has barely risen,' he says with a whimper. 'What have I got myself into?'

'A tournament that will not only better your game, but better yourself.'

'That's it. I'm out.' He draws back from the window. 'Go back to bed like a normal person.'

'I thought you were serious last night about wanting to prove everyone wrong,' I call out as he goes to close the window. 'Or am I wrong for believing in you?'

The window clicks shut and he disappears from view.

I wait a few seconds just in case my concluding words worked their magic and he's about to open the window again to tell me that I've inspired him enough to get down here, but nothing happens. Hanging my head, I sigh. This morning was always going to be a bit of a long shot. It's not like I'm that keen on a run right now, but the idea of getting Harley to join me propelled me out of bed earlier. In that moment, *he* was the motivation *I* needed.

Not that I'll ever tell him that.

I turn and walk back along his garden fence to the pavement and start out on my jog, taking it fairly easy. At first, I think I'm imagining the footsteps behind me, but as they get closer, I glance over my shoulder to see Harley in his T-shirt, shorts and running trainers jogging behind. I slow down, beaming at him as he approaches.

'Pick up the pace, Dawson,' he says with a grin, falling into step with me before edging forward. 'I thought you were serious about wanting to win.'

Laughing, I urge myself to go faster, overtaking him with ease, and giggling away at the surprise in his expression before he rushes to catch up.

By the time we get to the weekend before the J300 Roehampton – the junior grass tournament that takes place at the sports centre in Roehampton in the lead-up to the Wimbledon Championship – Harley and I have fallen into a routine.

We've been going for jogs together every morning before we train with Nick and encouraging each other through afternoon workouts or swims. Harley moaned a lot through the first couple of days, but I could see he was starting to get into it, and now I *know* that he enjoys it. A few days ago, I left the house first thing to find him waiting for me, leaning on the fence with a smug smile creeping across his face.

'About time,' he said as I strolled down the path to him. 'Had a nice lie-in, did we?'

'It's our usual time to run,' I said in confusion, checking my watch.

'I've already done my warm-up stretches,' he said with a sigh, tutting as I leaned on the fence for balance, kicking my foot back and reaching for it behind me for a quad stretch. 'Guess *some* of us are taking this more seriously than others.'

I scowled at him and then, the next day, I purposefully got up with loads of time to hurry out the house much earlier – where I was stunned to find him waiting for me yet again.

'I had a feeling you might want to retaliate today by making sure you'd be ready before me,' he remarked loftily, giving me an infuriatingly sympathetic smile. 'It was painful to get up even *earlier*, but being here right now to see *that* expression on your face –' he sighed, his grin growing wider – 'totally worth it.'

'You can be such a little shit, you know that, Harley?'

'Sticks and stones, Dawson.' He shrugged. 'I've just proven two things. One: you're absurdly competitive. And two—'

'You're a smug arsehole who likes to win as much as I do?' I huffed.

'*And two*,' he repeated, refusing to let me wipe that smile of his face, 'I know you better than you know yourself.'

I rolled my eyes and muttered something under my breath about how infuriating he was, but I had to fight a smile at the same time.

I have to admit to myself that I'm enjoying training with him, too.

Tom and I would practise together with Nick, but it's not like we needed to spend any more time together than we already did, so we'd go to the gym separately and unwind in our own ways without bothering one another. I'm so disciplined with my routine, I did worry that maybe in helping Harley find his, mine might suffer, but it's had the opposite effect. Having someone alongside me has improved my focus. I somehow feel more excited about the tournament now, more exhilarated about the idea of winning – it's like the challenge of it all has made me work harder and want the win even more than I already did.

And I think, in some weird way, Harley's presence relaxes me, too. With him around, I've started to laugh at myself a bit more, and that has turned out to be a good thing.

'What are you listening to?' he asked me during a gym session, leaning over on his exercise bike right next to mine to see what was up on my screen.

'It's a spin playlist on Spotify,' I told him through heavy breaths, taking out an earphone and slowing my pedalling. 'Why, what are you listening to?'

'The best song in existence for a workout.'

'Bold claim. What is it?'

'Put your earphone back in and close your eyes,' he instructed, reaching over to grab my phone, which was connected to my bike. 'I'm going to play it for you at the same time that I press play on mine.'

'Okay,' I chuckled, pressing my earphone back into place and shutting my eyes.

After a few seconds, the opening of 'Eye of the Tiger' by Survivor blasted into my ears.

I burst out laughing, opening my eyes to look at him. He was nodding his head along to the iconic guitar strumming, a dead serious expression on his face, before he began to punch the air to the beat. Turning to look at me, he broke into a grin and gestured for me to join him in jabbing our fists in front of us in rhythm to the music. Glancing nervously around at the other people in the gym, I shook my head and mouthed, '*No way.*' He looked insulted before mouthing, '*Do it*' back at me, leaning into his jabs with even more gusto. I rolled my eyes and relented, lifting my arms in a weak attempt at punching the air.

'*Yeah!*' he mouthed at me, his eyes lighting up, and his excitement spurred me on.

Soon the two of us were jabbing our fists in perfect coordination on our exercise bikes like absolute idiots, mouthing the words as we both got really into the song and pedalling faster without really thinking about it. It gave me a fresh burst of energy.

We've even impacted each other's downtime by lending one another books we think the other might like and recommending films to watch in the evenings. I started Stephen King's *The Dark Tower* series and was hooked from the first page, excited to discuss it with him over smoothies after a gruelling couple of hours of drills with Nick. I lent him my copy of *The Last Wish* by Andrzej Sapkowski and, despite the cynical raised eyebrows I got on handing him the book, he's admitted that he's loving it and is keen to read the rest of *The Witcher* series. I persuaded him to watch *La La Land* and he said he would if I watched it at the same time so that he wouldn't feel like he was watching a musical on his own, so we sat in our separate bedrooms in our adjacent houses whatsapping each other through the film.

> **Harley**
> This is actually really good

> **Billie**
> How are you surprised?
> It won so many Oscars

> **Harley**
> That doesn't mean a film is good

> **Billie**
> That's LITERALLY what the Oscars mean

Harley
Agree to disagree
Ryan sure can dance

Billie
Is it making you want to learn how to dance?

Harley
No
A little
Okay yes
I've googled local tap dance lessons
Want to join me?

Billie
I don't think I have time for tap

Harley
Everyone has time for tap
I'm signing us up
It could be good for our tennis
It's all rhythm and coordination
Basically what we do on the court

Billie
That's why so many tennis players have side careers in showbiz

Harley
You joke but I'm serious
I think I'll be naturally talented at tap too

Billie
Agree to disagree

Harley
You ever thought about dying your hair red?

Billie
Are you by any chance crushing on Emma Stone?

Harley
Big time
Bet she would join tap lessons with me

Billie
I don't think she needs any more lessons

Harley
Maybe I'll meet her in America
We can tap down the road together

Billie
Dream big, Harley

Harley
You know I do, Dawson
Clear your schedule Wednesday eve
That's our first beginners class
Wait
The instructor is called Lucy Foot
THAT CANNOT BE HER REAL NAME

Billie
You're joking, right?

Harley
I'm not joking!!
That's her GENUINE surname
And she teaches TAP DANCE
Her career was written in the stars

Billie
I meant, you're joking about

signing us up to tap dance, right?
RIGHT??

Harley
Oh
No
Don't worry, though
You can hire tap shoes if you don't have any

Billie
THE TAP SHOES ARE NOT
WHAT I'M WORRYING ABOUT

Harley
I'm excited about our new venture
First we dominate Wimbledon
Then we dominate the stage

'Very nice, you two,' Nick cries, clapping Harley and me as we high-five after beating Caleb and Scarlett in straight sets. 'You are ready for Roehampton on Monday.'

'I hope so,' I say, shaking our opponents' hands before we all make our way to the side of the court to grab our water bottles. 'It will be our first time playing together on grass, though.'

'Making it the perfect practice for Wimbledon the week

after,' Harley says, nudging me with his elbow. 'Don't bring us down, please, Dawson.'

'You're right,' I say, smiling apologetically. 'Bet we play even *better* on grass.'

'You know it,' he says, replacing the cap on his bottle.

'Huh,' Nick says, chuckling to himself.

'What?' I ask, confused. 'What's so funny?'

'Nothing's funny,' he says, his eyes drifting from me to Harley and back to me again. He breaks into a smile. 'I'm just glad I was right about something.'

CHAPTER FIFTEEN

Melrose's finest 💋🖤

> **Kat**
> GOOD LUCK, BILLIE!!
> We are so excited for today
> You are going to smash it
> LITERALLY
> Like, smash the ball

> **Jess**
> Good one, Kat

> **Kat**
> Thanks!!
> I'm so proud of myself
> And you, Bills!!

Jess
We really are
We can't wait to cheer you on

Billie
Thanks so much
I can't believe you're coming to watch
I'm very lucky to have you!!

Kat
We wouldn't miss it!!

Jess
And you won't be able to miss us
Seriously
Kat has made a sign for you
There is a LOT of glitter

Kat
It's gone everywhere
Bards's bedroom carpet now sparkles
He was fuming
Worth it though

Billie
Hahaha!
Aw thank you
You know Roehampton is low key, yeah?
There's no spectator stands
You watch at the sides of the courts
I don't want you to have grand expectations

Kat
Excuse me, it IS grand!
A proper tournament

Jess
We googled it and it looks amazing
Those smart grass courts are very fancy
Roehampton is for the REAL fans

Billie
That's true
I couldn't do this without you

Kat
We're with you all the way
Meeting Tom at the train station in a minute
How are you feeling?

Billie
Nervous

Jess
What are your digs like?

Billie
Nice, actually
Nick managed to get a good deal on a London hotel that's near Wimbledon
The atmosphere here is amazing

Jess
I bet
I hope you get to enjoy Wimbledon a bit

Billie
Wimbledon Village is buzzing
After I play, you two should check it out

> The pubs are always busy, especially during this first week of the main tournament

Jess
Ooh that's a good idea
What do you think, Kat?

Kat
I'll ask Bards
I said I'd hang with him later
But I can be late!

Jess
Yay! Got to make the most of Wimbledon

Billie
I've got to go warm up
See you at the courts!

Jess
You've got this
Good luck!

Kat
We love you!

My hands are trembling. I could tell I was getting inside my own head as I got ready in the locker room, intimidated by the other players milling around in there, so I came outside for some fresh air, standing to the side and watching other junior players come and go with their coaches as they made their way to and from courts.

I shouldn't be so nervous; as I said to Kat and Jess this morning, I won't be playing in front of crowds. While the juniors begin to battle it out at Roehampton this week, the whole world is focused on the famous grass courts fifteen minutes away, watching the first Monday of the Wimbledon Championships play out at the All England Lawn Tennis and Croquet Club. Here at the Roehampton courts, the real tension is between the juniors playing in the boys' and girls' singles tournaments, the young hopefuls planning on making their mark, winning an early title and increasing their ranking, just at the start of their career.

But not for me. For me, the doubles competition is all that matters.

This week at Roehampton is a chance to make my play on grass the best it can be, to analyse the competition we'll be facing next week at Wimbledon, to work out whether we really do have what it takes or whether we've been kidding ourselves like Bards said on Harley's first day of practice.

What if we lose today? The first day and we're knocked out. It could easily happen. Dad couldn't make it to watch the match because of work, but he did send me a message this morning wishing me luck. I can already hear his voice in my head when Tom relays the news that we crashed out of the first round: 'That's because you weren't there, son.' Tom's the winner, not me. It's never been me.

Exhaling a shaky breath, I crouch down to the ground, hanging my head and closing my eyes. I try to tell myself everything I need to hear: this is only one match. No matter what happens today, we still get to play on the Wimbledon courts next week. We have worked hard; we deserve to be here as much as anyone else. We can do this.

What if we can't do this? What if I can't do this? What if I let everyone down again and ruin the—

'Hey.'

I snap my head up at Harley's voice to find him crouching down opposite me, his eyes at the same level as mine. He reaches out to put a hand on my arm.

'You okay, Dawson?' he asks gently.

'Yeah. Yeah, course.' I fix a smile, standing up and pretending to brush something off my skirt while he straightens with me. 'I was . . . tying my lace.'

He tilts his head. 'You look a little shaky.'

'I'm not. I'm fine.'

'I know,' he says calmly. 'But if you are a little nervous, that's okay, too. A few nerves are a good thing. We need to be alert, ready for anything.'

I nod, my eyes falling to the ground.

'Hey,' he says softly, reaching out to hold my shoulders, my skin tingling beneath his warm grasp. I lift my gaze to find his eyes filled with concern. 'Talk to me.'

'I ... I'm fine. I was just ... I ...' My shoulders slump, my smile faltering, before I admit in a quiet voice, 'I'm scared.'

'Scared of what?'

'Failing. Again.'

There's a moment of silence before he says, 'Dawson, look at me.' He dips his head so I'm forced to look right into his eyes. His grip tightens on my arms. 'No matter what happens today, you have not failed. You haven't failed anyone, you haven't failed me, and most importantly, you haven't failed yourself.'

'If we lose—'

'Then we learn how to play better next time,' he says firmly. 'Losing now will make us more determined to win at Wimbledon. But we're not going to lose.'

'How do you know?' I ask, my voice quivering.

'I'm playing with the best doubles partner on the tour.'

I shake my head. 'I'm not the best player on the tour, Harley. The players in the singles tournaments are the real—'

'I didn't say you were the best player on the tour, Dawson,' he corrects, his lips curving into an easy smile. 'I said you were best *doubles partner*. That's different.'

I frown in confusion.

'We have the advantage here,' he continues, as though it's obvious. 'The others don't play together all the time like we've been doing. They're learning on the job. We already know how the other thinks and moves, what our strengths are and how to set the rallies up to play to them. Dawson, I've never known anyone to match you during a doubles game. You're not in it for yourself, and that is what makes you the best.'

I swallow, offering him a shaky smile. 'What makes *us* the best.'

'And there you have it,' he says triumphantly, dropping his hands. 'You think anyone else here is thinking like that? No way.'

'Maybe you're right.'

'You want to know something I've learned over the past couple of weeks?'

'How to tap dance?'

He chuckles. 'I don't think I can claim to have achieved that in one lesson, despite how much fun it was.'

'It really was fun,' I agree, breaking into a genuine smile as I recall how much the two of us laughed at the back of the studio while we tried to keep up with Lucy Foot.

In fact, I'm not sure I've laughed that much in a long time. I still can't believe that he managed to persuade me to attend that class, but I'm learning that Harley is very hard to say no to. Especially when he shoots you that winning smile, the one that makes his eyes crinkle.

'No, what I've learned is how to play not just for myself, but also for you,' he tells me. 'That's what I plan on doing today when we step out there on that court. You, Billie Dawson, have made me a team player. And I really like playing as a team. Don't you?'

'Yeah,' I say, nodding slowly. 'I do.'

'Then that's all we have to do today. Hopefully, we'll win some points as we go.' He hesitates. 'There's no one else I'd rather be with on that court, you know.'

He grins at me and my heart somersaults.

God, there it is. That smile. It's so achingly beautiful and his dark eyes so warm and sincere, they jumble my thoughts and make my breath catch in my throat.

'Ready?' he asks, jolting me out of my daze.

'Ready,' I confirm, before adding, 'thanks to you.'

'You can thank me by proving all of us right about your game on grass,' he says, turning to make his way to the practice court. 'It's where you really shine.'

As I follow him dutifully, a terrifying thought begins to niggle its way through from the back of my brain, something that I've been fighting to accept: that Harley is the only one I want to be with on that court today, too.

J300 Roehampton 2025 Mixed Doubles 1st Round
B. Dawson (GBR) & H. Pierce (GBR) vs
F. Russo (ITA) & S. Campbell (CAN)

Our opponents, Russo and Campbell, win the coin toss.

They choose to serve, Campbell holding out her hand for Russo to high-five before she makes her way back to the baseline while he crosses the court into position at the net.

Nick is standing in the pathway alongside the court, arms folded. There's an encouraging round of applause to the left where Tom, Kat and Jess are watching, Kat's sign that reads 'Go, Billie and Harley!' sparkling in the sunshine. It's hot today, the sun beating down on the courts. As Harley's up first to return at the baseline, I move towards the net on the left-hand side of the court. I glance back at him and he winks at me, flashing me that mischievous smile, spinning his racket in his hand.

Eyes forward, I bend my knees, doing everything I can to block the rest of the world out, my focus only on that yellow ball in Campbell's hand.

She bounces it on the ground. She tosses it high in the air. Her arm stretches. Her racket hits the ball, her body twisting as she follows through. The yellow blur zips past me, touching the right service line towards the centre, bouncing low and fast – too fast for Harley's racket to get there in time.

Ace.

'Fifteen–love.'

A smattering of lacklustre clapping. Blood is pounding in my ears. I spin round, making my way back to the baseline while Harley moves in, reaching out to tap my hand as we pass, a common doubles-partner gesture that's so small, but says everything: *Don't give up. We've got this. All that matters is the next point.*

Harley slows down long enough to mutter in a low, hurried voice, 'You can read her serve, Dawson. She has no variation on grass.'

He's right. I remember now. My nerves had blurred the memory of watching her practise this morning. She has a fast, powerful serve, but she's not confident on grass, that much was clear. Not like me. From the moment I started practising on grass yesterday, I felt like I was playing back where I was supposed to be.

Adjusting her cap, Campbell looks straight at me and then down as she bounces the ball. I steady my breathing, moving in a touch, crouching into position. Her serve is fast but flat and near the centre of the court again. As it bounces low, I'm there, returning it with a fast and powerful forehand, propelling her own force back against her. She had anticipated a shorter return and had moved in too soon. She gasps, jumping as the ball bounces at her feet forcing her to jump out of its way. She can't return it.

'Fifteen–all.'

I can hear Nick's strong, echoing clap and the cheers of my

brother and friends. When Harley turns round, he's giving me that smile, the one he wears when I've amused him without meaning to. We tap each other's hands in solidarity as we pass each other, my heart racing with the thrill of earning a point, electricity jolting up my arm from his touch.

There's no one else I'd rather be with on that court.

At the net, I grip the handle of my racket, bending my knees, breathing out slowly and steadily. Campbell serves to Harley and he's read it well this time, returning with a slice. Russo crosses the court to reach it, sending it back over the net into the right service area of our court, too far for me to get to, but Harley has run forward, tapping it over the net – the most beautiful, tidy little drop shot, the kind of risky play I'd rarely have the guts to attempt. But Harley always plays like he has nothing to lose.

'Fifteen–thirty.'

I jog back to the baseline. Campbell is irritated now. She's not going to lose her service game, not going to let us break this early. Under the visor of her cap, I can see her brow furrowed, her jaw locked. She angles her serve better this time and it takes me off guard, but I'm not giving up. I manage to return it, not brilliantly, but it goes up in the air and over the net deep enough for her to edge her way backwards, sending it back to me with an aggressive low backhand. It hits the top of the net but tips over onto the left service court of our side. A groan comes up from the row of spectators; Campbell holds her hand up.

'Thirty–all.'

Harley gives an *it happens* shrug as he passes me to prepare to return. Campbell looks less irked, but not relaxed. She knows that was a fluke, a stroke of luck. She can use it to her advantage, but she can't get complacent. Tossing the ball up in the air, she sends a serve straight into the net. My heart leaps. Harley moves in and she frowns. I glance over at Russo as he shuffles ever so slightly towards the doubles alley. Harley would have seen that too. He'll be reading Russo's anticipation of what's coming next: a ball to the outside of the service box rather than centred. He's right. She goes for a topspin serve bouncing neatly to the right of the box, much wider of the centre service line than she's done previously.

It could be a deceptive serve, but Harley's not fooled, and topspin is never as effective on grass. He sends it back with a topspin forehand of his own, one that she hasn't predicted.

'Thirty–forty.'

Shaking her head, Campbell moves to the other side of the court while Russo jogs back to whisper something to her before returning to the net. Harley gives me a sharp nod as our hands meet. *Game on.*

When Campbell serves a little slower than before down the line to my forehand, I have enough time to clock the gap down the centre of court that the two of them have left wide open. Swinging my racket back, I drive a huge amount of power into my groundstroke. I can tell from the satisfying punching sound the ball makes as it connects with the strings of my racket that it's going to land exactly where and how I want it to.

It whistles down the middle of them, bouncing near the baseline and out of play.

'Game, Dawson and Pierce.'

Jess and Tom cheer loudly, Kat's sign waving wildly above her head. I jog down to meet Harley at the net, holding out my hand to him.

'Not bad,' he utters quietly, grabbing my fingers and squeezing them briefly, 'and I can tell you're only getting started.'

I grin, desperate to prove him right.

We win the match in two straight sets.

CHAPTER SIXTEEN

J300 Roehampton 2025 Mixed Doubles 2nd Round
B. Dawson (GBR) & H. Pierce (GBR) vs
J. Bartos (CZE) & O. Benik (CZE)

We're down a set, but we shouldn't be. Bartos and Benik are great players individually, but they're barely communicating with each other, treating this almost like a practice match, not the real thing. Their indifferent attitude has thrown me off, making me tense and uneasy. I made too many unforced errors at the start, and now I'm scared to go for a winner. Playing it safe is something I've always been good at, and they can read me like a book: they're returning my serves with ease, predicting my moves, moving me round the court like a pawn. Harley is throwing in a few curveballs, but I know this is my fault.

I swig from my water bottle, furious at myself.

At least no one is here to see me fail. Tom has a doctor

appointment, since he hasn't been getting better, and I refused to let him change it. Jess and Kat offered to come, but Bards got pissed off at Kat for 'messing him around' after yesterday's match, so she said she had to go back to his. I think they had a big night with some of the Burton lot in the end. And thank goodness Dad isn't here. Our phone call last night was so positive, this would have made him regret everything he said.

'Well done, Billie – you've got the hard part out the way,' he told me. 'The first round is daunting. Tom tells me you played well.'

'I tried.'

'Sounds like you succeeded! Keep it up,' he said, joy fizzing through me as I heard the note of pride in his voice.

But here I am today, getting in my head, giving him nothing to be proud about.

'Did I ever tell you why I missed the final with you three years ago?' Harley says suddenly now, distracting me from my dismal thoughts.

I turn to look at him strangely, lowering my bottle. 'Huh?'

'The final at the club – you know, for that charity tournament,' he continues breezily, leaning back in his chair as though we're chilling at the jazz bar rather than sitting beside a Roehampton court about to lose an important match. 'I never told you what happened, did I?'

I shake my head.

'My mum was in an amateur production of Shakespeare's *The Winter's Tale*,' he says, his voice low and conspiratorial, 'and it was the matinée performance. Guess who drops out? The kid playing the bear.'

I blink at him. 'The ... *what*?'

'It's, like, Shakespeare's most famous stage direction: "*Exit, pursued by a bear.*"' Harley sighs. 'And the guy playing the bear messages the morning of the show saying that he has to rain check because he's booked a driving lesson that he doesn't want to miss. All the cast are in a panic, so what does Mum do? She asks me to step in. No, not asks. Tells.'

'Time,' the umpire says.

Harley rises from his seat. I do the same, picking up my racket, enraptured.

'She didn't care that I was playing in the tournament. She tells me that if I don't put on that bear suit, I'm going to be in big trouble – there might be agents in the audience; she needs this show to go well,' he says, strolling onto the court. 'So, I have a choice to make: piss her off and go and play with you in the charity tournament, making my home life a guaranteed living hell, or play the role of a bear in a truly terrible amateur production that slaughtered Shakespeare's work.'

We stop at the service line.

'And that, Dawson,' he says, a playful smile spreading across his face, 'is how I found myself later that day in a boiling hot, stinky bear suit, waddling across the stage going, "Roar" and falling flat on my face in front of an audience of about twenty people.'

I burst out laughing.

He points his racket at me. 'I've missed that smile. Right. Come on, give them hell.'

With that, he moves to his position at the net. I'm up to serve. Selecting two balls, I'm still marvelling at how I thought he'd sacked me off all those years ago because he simply couldn't be bothered to care. As I bounce the ball, focusing on where I'm going to place the serve, I feel a little lighter. The weight on my heart has lifted, the pressure easing as the laughter from his story bubbled up my throat. I don't rush to serve; I take my time. A vision of him in a bear suit totters across my brain. I smile before tossing the ball high, dropping my racket and swinging it up through the air to chase it.

Ace.

At the net, Harley straightens and swaggers across the court, glancing back to mouth, '*Roar*' at me, his eyes flashing with mischief. Shaking my head, I chuckle and move along the baseline to the other side.

We win that set seven games to six on a tie-break.

We win the third set six games to two.

J300 Roehampton 2025 Mixed Doubles Semi-Finals
B. Dawson (GBR) & H. Pierce (GBR) vs
K. Takei (JPN) & J. Singh (IND)

Harley and I sail through the quarter-finals, but Takei and Singh, who we face in the semis, are our toughest opponents yet. They fight for every single point, and while Takei may be better on clay, Singh is born to play on grass. You can tell how much he loves this surface, his fierce energy radiating from him at every point.

We scraped through to win the first set seven games to six on a tie-break. But they've taken the second set in record time at six games to two. It's as though they needed to lose the first one to really bring out the fight in them. I don't know whether we're going to be able to come back from this; it's the penultimate day of the tournament and my confidence is shot; my muscles are aching. It's been a big week.

I sigh heavily, unable to bring myself to look up at Tom, who is standing with Nick at the side of the court. Tom has been so supportive this week, showing up to matches when he can, messaging me every day before the start of my matches, telling me that I can do this. It must be hard for him to stand at the side and watch helplessly, knowing that he should have been a part of this. Dad said he'd try to make it tomorrow if I made the finals, but that's hardly looking likely.

'Let's make this interesting,' Harley says in a low voice,

leaning forward to rest his elbows on his knees as he glances around the court.

I dab my damp forehead with my towel. 'How?'

'A bet.'

'What do you mean?' I ask, dropping my towel on my lap and leaning forward to grab my energy drink from the ground.

'If we lose, we go skinny-dipping in the hotel pool tonight,' Harley suggests.

I turn to him wide-eyed. 'No way! I'm not doing that. No bet.'

'Hang on, I haven't finished the full terms and conditions yet,' he says, leaning back in his chair and folding his arms. 'If we lose, we go skinny-dipping in the hotel pool. And if we win, I will reprise my role of Bear in the hotel bar in front of everyone.'

I blink at him.

He nods slowly, as though accepting his fate. 'If I can track down a bear suit this afternoon, I will do it tonight. Otherwise, I will do it at some point this weekend. Yes, Dawson, you heard me correctly. If we win, I run through the hotel going, "*Roar*."'

'With gusto? You'd do it properly?'

He looks insulted. 'I promise to roar my little heart out.'

I can't fight a smile. 'Oh my god. I would love to see that.'

'So –' he holds out his hand – 'do we have a deal?'

Pressing my lips together, I eye up his hand warily. There's a lot at stake here – the idea of skinny-dipping sends a shiver of horror down my spine ... although I wouldn't be alone. Harley would be with me. And with a few drinks down me, I reckon I could just about bring myself to do it. I bite my lip.

'Time,' comes the voice of the umpire.

Harley stands up, his hand still outstretched. I push myself up off my chair and take his hand in mine, shaking it.

'I'm not sure you've thought this through, Harley,' I say, as we bend down to pick up our rackets. 'Either way, you lose.'

'How did you get there?'

'If we win, you're in a bear suit, and if we lose, we're skinny-dipping.'

'Exactly,' he says proudly, spinning the grip of his racket in his hand. 'If we win, we're through to the finals and I couldn't give a shit what I have to wear. And if we lose, then I'm swimming naked with you tonight. Sounds like a win-win to me.'

He flashes me a grin, balancing his racket over his shoulder as he nonchalantly strolls to our end of the court.

Later that evening, I take a deep breath, my stomach twisting with nerves.

I can't believe this is happening. Fucking hell, this is embarrassing.

But a bet is a bet.

'You ready?' I ask Harley, biting my lip.

'Oh yeah,' he says, his eyes wide with excitement.

'Okay.' I exhale. 'Let's do this.'

Giving me a salute, Harley shoves the bear mask over his head.

I break into a wide smile, stepping back to admire the full bear outfit. The hotel receptionist is watching us, his jaw on the floor.

'See you on the other side, Dawson,' he says, his voice muffled.

'Break a leg, Harley.'

Lifting his furry paws in the air, his 'ROAR' echoes around the walls before he lumbers across the reception and through the hotel bar, stunning the guests into silence with his energetic performance. I can't stop giggling, clapping as enthusiastically as possible and cheering at the top of my lungs.

CHAPTER SEVENTEEN

'A toast,' I declare, holding my glass of sparkling water and lemon aloft. 'To the best performance of Bear in Shakespeare's stage direction "*Exit, pursued by a bear*" that I've ever seen. May this be the beginning of a long and successful bear career.'

Harley knocks his glass against mine. 'Thank you, Dawson. I'm glad you appreciate fine theatre when you see it.'

We sip our drinks. Thanks to Harley's surprise bear stint, the barman in the hotel offered us any drink on the house and, when we said that tonight they had to be soft drinks, he said he'd put our free drinks on hold so, whatever the result of tomorrow's match, we'd have a strong drink waiting for us when we got back.

The barman's reaction was certainly better than that of the hotel manager, who said very politely that, although the performance was extremely entertaining, he would prefer it if we didn't do anything like that again during our stay.

I put down my drink. 'I can't believe you just did that.'

'I don't back out of a bet.'

'You are braver than I am.'

He lifts his eyebrows in surprise. 'Are you telling me you wouldn't have skinny-dipped tonight in the pool if we'd lost the match?'

'No, I would have done it,' I say with conviction.

'See? A bet is a bet. Nothing you can do. Got to roll with the punches.' He pauses, his eyes fixing on me. 'And it's easier to make a fool of yourself when you have a cheerleader.'

'I'm not sure you needed me cheering for you tonight.'

'Yes, I did.'

My face flushes with heat under his intense gaze. I reach forward to pick my glass up again, looking for something to do.

'We're through to the final tomorrow. Feels surreal,' I note, taking a sip.

'We've proven that we're ready to take on everyone at Wimbledon next week.'

'There will be other doubles partners we haven't played against yet taking part in Wimbledon – overall the competition will be tougher,' I point out. 'And our previous opponents will have had more practice on grass by then.'

'So will we,' he counters, tilting his head at me. 'Have you seen the article on the ITF website this afternoon that includes our win today?'

'Yeah, Nick sent me the link.'

'Then you know they described you as a *"fierce powerhouse on grass"*.'

'And they described you as *"swift and nimble"*.'

He laughs lightly. 'Yeah, I liked that.'

'It makes you sound like an elf in *Lord of the Rings*.'

He clicks his fingers at me. 'The elves are cool, right?'

'Very cool.'

He hesitates, before asking carefully, 'Did you read the comment the journalist made about wondering why he hadn't seen you more on the junior singles circuit?'

'I did.'

'Is it okay for me to tell you I've been wondering the same thing?'

I look at him in surprise. 'Really?'

'I've thought about it for a while now,' he admits, creases appearing across his forehead. 'Can I ask why?'

'Sure – I mean, it's an easy answer. I wasn't good enough.'

He peers across the table at me. 'You're kidding. You really think that?'

'It's not what I think; it's what I know. If anyone was ever going to be the tennis star in our family, it was Tom. He's the one who had all the talent, but ... I don't know. Guess he wasn't quite good enough, either.'

'Billie, you are as good as anyone in the juniors, and you've always been just as good as Tom, if not better. You could have gone pro if you'd wanted. If you'd gone to Florida and trained there, or—'

'Harley,' I interrupt, smiling at him, 'I appreciate you trying to big me up, but it's okay. I made my peace with it long ago. I love tennis so much and maybe . . .' I sigh heavily. 'Maybe in another life I would have taken a chance and tried to make it, but in the end I wasn't good enough physically or mentally in my early teens when you have to make those decisions. All the stuff with Mum . . . my head wasn't in the right place, and Tom and I could never have left Dad on his own and trained abroad or moved around the world with the tour.'

Harley nods slowly. 'Well, for what it's worth, I don't think it's because you weren't good enough. It's because you chose not to.'

'Thanks. Hey, I still get to play all the time,' I remind him. 'So it's not like my passion for the sport dampened. And I plan on playing for a long time.'

'The University of East London has a good team?'

'Uh, *yes*,' I say, unable to stop a laugh of surprise that he doesn't know this. 'UEL has one of the best university tennis teams in the country. They have a few ATP-ranked players and loads of BUCS medal winners.'

'What is BUCS?'

'The British Universities and Colleges Sport championships,' I tell him eagerly. 'That was the whole reason I wanted to go to UEL. Sure, a degree would be nice, but the tennis team is the main drive.'

'They won't know what's hit them when you show up.'

'UEL kicks butt in the doubles tournaments, too,' I note, shooting him a look. 'You haven't applied for a university yet, right?'

'I'm waiting for my results first.'

'Maybe UEL could be added to your list, then.'

The corners of his mouth twitch upwards. 'Are you saying you would like me to come to the same university as you, Dawson?'

'If it means we can continue dominating the doubles courts, then I wouldn't mind.'

He swirls the liquid round his glass. 'Is that the only reason?'

Our eyes lock. I shift in my seat, clearing my throat.

'Your natural tennis talent is obviously the main draw,' I say with a wry smile. 'But I guess you're all right to hang out with, too.'

I expect him to laugh, but he doesn't. Instead, he studies me. It's so rare that I see Harley's serious side that when I do, I instantly feel on edge, suddenly self-conscious. Like he can see straight through me.

'You're not too bad yourself, Dawson,' he says eventually, not taking his eyes off me.

I feel flustered and nervous, fidgeting with the hem of

my denim shorts. In contrast, he's calm and collected, his expression set. He looks focused and sure. I recognize his expression and stance from the countless times I've seen it on the court.

I've seen it when he's made up his mind that he's going to win the next point.

We stop outside my room. The hotel corridor is empty and silent. I swipe my room key and the door clicks open. I step inside and turn to face Harley, holding the door open with my foot. It's been such a fun evening, I didn't want to come upstairs to bed yet, but after our second soft drink at the bar, we both accepted that we should get an early night with such a big day looming over us.

Harley puts his hands in his pockets, lingering at my door.

I wonder if he doesn't want to quite finish the evening yet, either.

'Great performance today,' I say, my heart thudding against my chest.

'You too.'

'I was talking about the bear.'

He breaks into a smile. 'Like I said, I couldn't have done it without you.'

I chuckle and then we fall into silence. I should say goodnight and close the door, but something is stopping me – a pull that I can't seem to shut down.

'Well,' he says eventually, bringing his eyes up to meet mine, 'goodnight, then.'

'Night,' I say quietly, an ache tugging in my chest.

He steps forward and leans in, dipping his head to kiss me on the cheek.

He's never done that before, we've never been this close before, and my breath hitches as I breathe in his cologne, a warmth pooling in my stomach, my skin burning beneath his lips. He doesn't pull back straight away, his cheek hovering next to mine. My willpower snaps. I know exactly what I'm doing when I turn my head ever so slightly to angle my mouth up towards his.

And Harley doesn't hesitate.

His lips brush against mine, softly and tentatively at first. I close my eyes as I melt into him, the air whooshing out of my lungs, my arms reaching around the back of his neck. As I arch my back into him, I give him the permission he needs to deepen the kiss, his warm, strong hands finding my waist and pulling me closer to him, his tongue sliding against mine and setting off sparks in my chest. When I tangle my fingers through his hair, he groans into my mouth, the kiss growing frantic and urgent as he moves me into my room, shutting the door behind us and pinning me up against it. He breaks the kiss for a moment to look at me, our breathing fast and shallow.

'Fuck, Billie,' he whispers, his eyes blazing with heat.

I manage a shy smile before he crashes his mouth against

mine again. I've never been kissed like this, like he's scared to lose it now we're here. I've never felt so *needed* like this.

And I've never wanted anyone so much.

God, I want him. I'm completely and utterly intoxicated by him. The way he tastes, the way he smells, the warmth of his body pressed against mine. I can't pinpoint the moment I started wanting to be kissed by Harley Pierce, but I have a feeling it's a long time before now, longer than I'd care to admit. He's not holding back any more and neither am I. His hands are everywhere, roaming down my waist, over my hips. I moan against his lips, desperate for more of him, all of him, and the sound ignites something in him because he kisses me even harder, my hands cupping his strong jaw while his move to my waist. He wrenches up my white tank top that's tucked into my high-waisted shorts so he can slide his hands beneath the fabric, the warmth of his touch covering my skin in goosebumps.

I can barely breathe.

I'm aching for him, gasping at his lips, pressing my hips into his, my hands moving down to his broad shoulders, my nails digging into the taught skin of his muscles. As I slide my fingers over his solid chest, feeling my way down every ridge and dip of his abs to the hem of his T-shirt, he breaks the kiss to press his forehead against mine.

'You have no idea how long I've wanted this,' he whispers with a low, shaky breath.

My heart flutters, my chest expanding with the surge of

longing I feel for him as he looks up at me beneath those long, full eyelashes. He's so pretty. So unbelievably beautiful. And he makes me feel like I can do anything. He looks at me like I continually amaze him. *Me.* The person who's always been second best, never believing I could amaze anyone.

He brushes his fingers gently across my cheekbone, brushing my hair back to tuck it behind my ear before his lips find mine again.

There's a knock on my door.

We freeze.

'Billie? You in there?' Nick says.

Harley draws back, his hands dropping to his side. I close my eyes, agonized.

'Yeah, I'm here,' I say, my voice croaky and uneven. 'I'm ... in bed. Everything okay?'

'All good. I'm checking my star players are getting their beauty sleep. You seen Harley? I've knocked on his door, but he's not answering.'

I glance up at him and we both break into a guilty smile. I have to clasp a hand over my mouth to stop myself from giggling, and Harley grabs my hips to pull me close to him again, kissing my forehead and whispering, 'Shh,' his breath tickling my skin.

'No, I haven't seen him. Maybe he's already asleep,' I call back, before pressing my lips against his neck, smiling to myself as I hear Harley sigh.

'Maybe. Okay, well sleep well,' Nick says. 'Big day tomorrow. The biggest yet. Make sure you get a good night's sleep. You have to be well rested.'

'Night, Coach.'

We hear his footsteps fade away down the corridor, listening out for the sound of his door opening and then shutting before we dare to speak. Harley exhales, keeping hold of my hips but taking a step back.

'I really don't want to say this, but—'

'But, Nick's right. We should get an early night,' I finish for him, my heart crying out in despair as my head comes back into control.

Harley nods, lifting a hand to rake his fingers through his hair. '*Fuck*.'

He looks at me, his jaw tensing. I step free of his other hand, folding my arms across my body self-consciously. I feel suddenly cold and exposed without him close.

'I'll ... see you tomorrow,' he says hoarsely.

'See you tomorrow,' I mutter, attempting a weak smile as my eyes fall to the floor, too embarrassed and awkward to look at him.

Then his hand is at my chin, gently tilting my mouth up towards him, his other moving to the small of my back as he kisses me, an achingly slow kiss that sends a shiver rolling down my spine.

Then he draws back and turns to leave, pausing at the door

to glance back and smile at me before he quietly slips out. The door shuts behind him and I'm left alone, leaning back against the wall and desperately trying to steady my breathing and slow my heart rate. But it's no use. *I like Harley Pierce.* A lot. And I have no idea how I'm going to get any sleep when all I can think of is the way he kissed me.

CHAPTER EIGHTEEN

All morning, I've been telling myself to focus on the tennis. But my thoughts keep running away from me, sending jolts of electricity through my entire body as I remember Harley's hands roaming all over my body, my hands threading through his thick, dark hair, the taste of his lips on mine ...

I think about what he said and my heart races: *You have no idea how long I've wanted this.*

My head is all over the place. I'm terrified that we've let this happen, worried about how it will play out next, furious that it may affect our game when we've come so far. But I'm also excited and alert, giddy with joy when I think about him. This could make us play together even better, because there's no way now that I want to disappoint him. Like he said, we're playing for each other, too.

I practically skip down to breakfast, but I don't see him there. In fact, when I meet Nick in the lobby, he tells me that Harley is already at the courts. He went out early this morning and messaged Nick to let him know that he'd meet us there.

A pang of worry flickers in my chest. But I brush it aside. He can't be avoiding me. That would be stupid. We're playing in the finals of a tournament together today, and we're playing as a doubles team all of next week at Wimbledon. There's so many reasonable explanations as to why he's not here this morning. Maybe he slept badly and didn't want to hang around. He might have wanted to practise alone for a bit before I got there, which is understandable – sometimes I prefer to hit against the ball machine and get warmed up before taking on a person; it's more reliable for placing groundstrokes.

By the time I'm in the car on the way to the courts, I've managed to convince myself that everything is fine. When I'm in the girls' locker room getting ready, I take a moment to read through the messages from my dad – he's cleared his calendar just like he promised. He's on his way with Tom. I try to calm my nerves at the prospect of him watching the match by reading through the messages from Jess and Kat, only to feel a little disappointed.

Group chat: Melrose's finest 🌿♥

Kat
Billie, I'm so so sorry but I can't come to the match today

Kat
Bards has surprised me with tickets to this funfair in east London!
I've tried to work out how to go to both, but it's literally on the other side of the city

Jess
What?! Nooooo!
Can't you go to the fair over the weekend?
It can't only be on today, right?

Kat
I've tried, but the tickets are just for today!
And he says he can't get a refund
I'm so sorry, but I promise I'll be in the queue for a Wimbledon ground pass on Monday

Billie
Don't worry, Kat, I totally understand!
Wimbledon is the important bit
Have fun today!

Kat
You're the best

> Good luck, you'll be amazing
>
> Jess, cheer big enough for the both of us!!

> **Jess**
> You know it
> See you soon, Bills
> You've got this xxx

Putting my phone away, I zip up my sports jacket and sling my tennis bag over my shoulder, ready to head out to the practice courts. Coming out of the building, I happen to glance over to the right and I double-take, stopping abruptly.

Harley is standing there, talking to a girl.

He's got his back to me, but I know it's him. I recognize her from the junior singles circuit: her name is Grace Lewis, a fellow Brit. She's smiling up at him, her bright green eyes sparkling, her pearly-white teeth on full display as she laughs at something he says. I watch as he reaches out to her neck, brushing her glossy brown hair out the way to carefully lift the gold pendant hanging on her necklace, admiring it as she tilts her head, her lips forming a natural pout while gazing up at him. She says something and he nods, lowering his hand.

A lump rises in my throat as any doubt is swiftly swept away when she reaches into her pocket and pulls out her phone, handing it to him.

He takes it, adding his number into her contacts.

Turning on my heel before they see me, I rush back into the building, knocking into someone coming out and frantically apologizing to them before hurrying into the girls' toilets and locking myself in a cubicle. I lean back against the door.

I scrunch up my face, desperately trying not to cry. What the fuck is wrong with me? I *know* what Harley Pierce is like. I've always known. And I still managed to fall for his bullshit. I promised myself I'd always be smarter than that. I considered myself lucky to know him for who he was, satisfied that I'd never be caught in his trap. I felt sorry for the girls he would ensnare with his good looks, charm and easy conversation, before he'd drop them for whoever was unfortunate enough to catch his eye next. How arrogant could I have been to think that I could change that? That I might be enough for him.

What. An. Idiot.

My heart is hammering against my chest so hard, the blood is pounding in my ears. My face is flushed hot with humiliation. Tears prick at the back of my eyes and I can't hold them back completely. One streaks down my cheek and I almost crumple, a small sob escaping from my throat before I can stop it.

This hurts a bit more than I thought it would.

We've been in a bubble these last few weeks, me and Harley. He's become a big part of my life; someone I've come to rely on; someone who brings me up when I feel down; someone who I talked to about things that I've never really confessed to anyone. I thought we were friends, but after last night, I let myself believe we were more than that. I've admitted to myself that I like him. We've spent so much time together that I mistook our connection, the chemistry on court, for something *real*.

I can't believe I let myself fall for him.

Oh my god, this is so embarrassing. So fucking mortifying. Those words I've been playing in my head all night and all morning, the words that I thought were what I wanted to hear: *You have no idea how long I've wanted this.* I thought he said that because he'd liked me for longer than I knew. But what he meant was that I had kept him at a distance, refusing to be a conquest, and he had taken the challenge and finally won.

I've been well and truly played.

Tearing off some toilet tissue, I dab at my face, collecting myself. I'm not going to let this disrupt what I've worked so hard for. I will not let a boy distract me from what I want; I never should have let last night happen. Thank god Nick interrupted us.

My focus has always been on winning at Wimbledon next week, and that's exactly what I'm going to do. I won't hate Harley, because that might affect our teamwork. When I really think about it, he's done nothing wrong. We're not exclusive; we've had *one* kiss. It was nothing. He's allowed to go out and flirt with whoever he wants. That's got nothing to do with me. All I care about is how he plays on the court. And maybe I can turn any ... frustration about him into a positive. I will channel my anger and hurt into my game. Harley can do what he wants. I can do what I want.

And what I want is to win. Nothing else matters.

He matters, a small voice says at the back of my brain.

But I don't matter to him. I know that now. *I don't matter to him.*

Scrunching the toilet paper up in a ball in my hand, I toss it down the loo and then exit the cubicle, marching out the bathroom with only one thing on my mind: tennis.

Because nothing else matters.

J300 Roehampton 2025 Mixed Doubles Finals
B. Dawson (GBR) & H. Pierce (GBR) vs
G. Jackson (USA) & C. Cox (USA)

They're too good.
We're not good enough.
We're going to lose.

Wiping the beads of sweat off my forehead with the back of my hand, I place my left foot up against the baseline and bounce the ball to serve. The grass beneath my feet is worn now; the ground is brown and dusty. The ball thuds against it. Once. Twice. Three times.

I'm so tired.

Tossing the ball in the air, I swing my racket up and over to meet it, following through to watch it sail straight into the net. As the ball boy runs to pick it up before returning to crouch at the side of the net, I get back into position. I bounce the ball. Once. Twice. Three times. I'll go for a kick serve this time. It's slower, but it's unpredictable – the spin might confuse them – although they seem to be able to predict every move I make. I knew they were going to be hard to beat. Cox and Jackson have played together a while, they're friends, and they've blitzed their competition this week. Cox has astounding power, and Jackson is so agile and sharp with her tactics, a chess master playing on her very own board. They won their semi-finals draw six–one, six–one.

And they took the first set against us six games to three.

I toss the ball up and . . . panic. It's not a good toss. I should let the ball fall back down, apologize and go again. I have a split second to make that decision. I don't let it go. I swing my racket up over my head and hit the ball into the net.

Double fault. My first of the second set. My second of the match.

Out of the corner of my eye, I watch my dad run his hand down his face, grimacing behind it. He knows what I know. I've bottled it. We cannot beat this brilliant American duo. We are not good enough.

'Love–forty.'

Shit.

Through a smile, Harley is mouthing something to me as he moves across the court at the net for the next point. I look away, not wanting to know what he's trying to tell me. I don't need his reassurance or his pity. I don't want anything from him but for him to pull his weight when the rally begins – that's all I'm asking for. That's all any doubles partner wants. As I resign myself to the loss, I try not to lose all hope. I start to plot what I'll say to Dad after the match to convince him not to give up on me yet: *'This isn't Junior Wimbledon – it's not the tournament win I'm really after. This is a warm-up. I should have conserved my energy for next week. That's why I didn't fight back like I could have done . . .'*

Still, I should try and get one point during my service game.

Harley crouches low. I bounce the ball on the ground – once, twice, three times – and toss it up in the air, a perfect toss, before striking with full power. It's a fast serve. Jackson isn't as prepared for it as she thinks, but she returns it with a weak backhand cross-court. Racing forward, I send it back with a slice backhand, keeping my momentum going by moving up to the net. Jackson reaches the ball, lobbing it over Harley's head. He rushes back to square up to it at the baseline as it bounces high in the air, greeting the ball as it falls with a forehand that lacks the power we need to win the point. I exhale in frustration.

When Jackson sends it back, I dive for it, unwilling to rely on Harley. It's just within my reach, my volley punching the ball over the net. Cox reacts with lightning speed, lunging to meet it before it bounces, placing it in the open space I've just vacated.

'Game, Jackson and Cox.'

Bollocks.

Balling my free hand into a fist, I drift to the side of the court, ignoring Harley's puzzled expression. He'll be wondering why I took a ball that surely should have been his. I won't apologize for it. During the changeover, Harley tries to make me laugh with some anecdote, but I cut him off.

'Sorry, Harley, I'm trying to focus on the match,' I say flatly, looking straight ahead.

He stares at me, stunned into silence. But he should know that this isn't the time for personal stories. We're not here to get to know each other better; we're here to play.

We lose the J300 Roehampton Final six–three, six–two.

As I walk in silence back to the locker rooms, Nick falls into step with me and says brightly that we learned a lot from that match. Cox and Jackson have shown us their strengths, but also their weaknesses, and we will come back stronger next week.

Once I've showered, I sit for a moment in my towel on the bench in the middle of the changing room, staring at nothing.

My phone vibrates with a call from Tom. He tells me that he's waiting outside, but Dad had to rush off for a meeting – he did hang around as long as he could, but he couldn't get out of this one. Tom passes on the message from him that he'll call me later and he's very proud. I don't doubt for a second that Tom has embellished his words.

I sit in my towel for a long time. Long enough so that when I finally emerge dressed and ready to go back to the hotel, Harley has already left.

CHAPTER NINETEEN

Jess
I hope you're out having a drink right now

Billie
Yes, don't worry
Nick has forced us out to one of the pubs in Wimbledon Village
I am consoling myself with vodka, soda lime

Jess
You should be CELEBRATING

Billie
You were there today
You saw me lose

Jess
I saw you in the final of a big tournament
I saw you play amazingly
You should celebrate how far you've come
Both of you!

> **Billie**
> You're sweet
> How's the party?
> Is Kat there yet?

Jess
Yes, she got here with Bards about half an hour ago

> **Billie**
> Did they have a good time at the fair?

Jess
I think so
He's acting a bit weird

> **Billie**
> Weird how?

Jess
I might be wrong but there's a girl here
She and Bards seem ... close

Billie
What?
Really??

Jess
When Kat wasn't in the room, he was kind of all over her
He didn't see me in there too

Billie
Are you sure they were flirting?
Could she just be a friend?

Jess
Not from where I was standing
My gut tells me there's more

Billie
What a dick
Are you going to tell Kat?

Jess
What can I say?
That I saw him talking to another girl???
I may have read the room wrong
Kat will think I'm meddling

Billie
I don't trust him

Jess
Me neither
Kat and I had a bit of a fight earlier

Billie
You never fight!?

Jess
Apparently we do now
I said that Bards never lets her go out with anyone else any more and it's a bit weird
I think I went too far
She bit my head off
She said I should be happy for her
Which I am!
I've apologized but . . .
Things still feel awkward
Anyway, wish you were here

Billie
I wish that too
You were looking out for her
It's what friends do
Even if it makes things awkward
She knows that

Jess
Yeah
Look, do me a favour?

Billie
Anything

Jess
Try to enjoy tonight
Raise a glass to you for me

Billie
I'll try
Hey, you do me a favour too
Look after Kat
Even if it's fucking awkward

Jess
Always x

The Dog and Fox in Wimbledon Village is filled with tennis fans, tourists and locals, all of whom are in such high spirits that it's near impossible to feel down among them. Bathed in the orange glow of the Friday evening sun, the beer garden is busy and Nick has secured a great table in the middle of it. With the upbeat music playing in the background, surrounded by people chatting, laughing, buzzing with excitement as the first week of the Wimbledon Championships draws to a close, I find myself unable to stay upset about our loss today for too long.

Part of that is also down to Harley, a fact I begrudgingly accept.

I've been trying to make sure that I don't engage with him in any manner that wouldn't be perceived as strictly professional. I've been probing Nick about the mistakes we made today and how we can improve, but even he got tired of the tennis talk and insisted we spend 'at least one evening relaxing'.

I can tell that Harley has been puzzled by my change in behaviour, but he hasn't been overzealous in trying to bring me back around. Maybe he suspects that I saw him with Grace. Or maybe he thinks I'm regretting what happened last night, regardless of who else he's messing around with, and he doesn't want to complicate things by pretending he cares.

Ever since the match, he's been acting ... well ... normal. Which is probably a good thing. Despite whatever tension is running between us, we do still have next week to get through, and we're going to have to find common ground. If he stays like this – calm, easy-going, fun – and we pretend like last night never happened, I think I'll be able to work with him. We'll be fine. All I have to do is pretend not to be hurt. Pretend like I never fell for him in the first place.

Which is easier said than done. When Nick gets up to go to the toilet, I don't know where to look, glancing around the beer garden, eager for distraction. Harley is not thinking along the same lines. I can feel his dark eyes boring into me.

'Did you see the wall of bookshelves in the pub on your way through?' he asks, cutting through the silence Nick left us in.

'Sure.'

'You know why they're there?'

'Because people like to sit in cosy pubs and read books?' I mutter, fiddling with the corner of a beer mat.

'Not just *any* people. Fred Perry used to sit in the armchair by that wall and read books to unwind during the championships. Apparently, he liked fantasy fiction best.'

I snap my head up to look at him. 'Seriously?'

He grins at me. I roll my eyes.

'Okay, I'm annoyed I fell for that,' I grumble, picking up my glass.

'I'm not. It got you to look at me at least.' He fixes his eyes on mine. 'Hey, Billie.'

Averting my gaze, I don't say anything, taking a large gulp of my drink.

Nick returns, weaving through the crowded garden to stand at the end of the table, placing two more drinks down in front of us.

'Right, you two, I'm off to go for dinner with Seb,' he announces, checking his watch.

'He's in Wimbledon?' I say with surprise. 'I didn't see him today.'

'He travelled in after work this evening to take me out,' Nick explains.

'Thanks for the invite, Uncle Seb,' Harley remarks sarcastically.

Nick gives him a look. 'Funnily enough, I didn't think an eighteen-year-old would be all that keen to spend Friday night at a dinner with his two uncles. And, no offence, but I haven't seen my husband all week and I'm not sure I want to spend our one evening together in the company of two teenagers.'

'Offence taken,' Harley declares.

Nick points his finger sternly at both of us. 'I bought you these drinks as your final round, got it? After this, get back to the hotel and get some rest. We have a big weekend of training ahead of us if we're going to have you in shape for Wimbledon.'

'Thanks, Coach,' I say, finishing off the last of my previous drink and sliding the new one towards me. I can already feel the vodka making me more relaxed.

Harley nods to Nick before he leaves us to it, battling his

way out of the beer garden and hailing a taxi. Harley turns back to me.

'And then there were two. Right, I'd like to raise a glass to you,' he announces.

'What for?'

'For getting me here. I wasn't sure I'd make it this far.' He hesitates, his hand still holding up his glass expectantly. 'I always knew *you* would, though.'

The muscles around my mouth betray me, fighting to lift into a smile.

I lose the battle, sighing as I clink my glass against his.

He's annoyingly good at winning me over. *As a tennis partner*, the sensible part of my brain reminds me. *Nothing more.*

'I'm happy for you,' I say, taking a sip.

'For us.' He puts his glass down, leaning both elbows on the table. 'And look, today was always going to be a tough match, but we can come back stronger next week.'

'I know.'

'Good.' He grins at me. 'Ask me what happened to me today—'

'You landed a hot date with a junior star?' I reply bitterly, quick as a flash.

Confusion flits across his expression. 'No,' he says slowly, squinting at me as though I've said something outrageous. I have another sip of my drink. 'No, Dawson, after the match today, I accidentally gave away my tennis racket.'

I blink at him. 'What?'

'I *gave away* my tennis racket,' he repeats, exhaling all the air from his cheeks, his eyes growing wide. 'Nick is going to kill me.'

Against all my best efforts to stop it, a laugh escapes from my throat. 'Sorry, hang on. How do you ... accidentally give away your racket?'

'You know Jason Woodford?'

'Of course, the American player. He won Wimbledon twice.'

'And he now coaches one of the juniors,' he tells me. 'He was outside the building chatting to someone, carrying his tennis bag, and this kid went up to him and asked if he could get a photo with him holding one of his rackets. Jason said no.'

My mouth drops open. 'He said no? Poor kid.'

'Exactly my thoughts. Jason walked off and the boy looked embarrassed, so I strolled over to him, got my racket out of my bag and handed it to him. I said, "Take this."'

'Okay.'

'His face lit up, and he said, "Really?" and I said, "Sure." He thanked me and then he literally ran off with it. I stood there and watched him go. I thought he might come back, but ... he didn't.'

'Harley.' I close my eyes for a moment in despair, rubbing my forehead with my fingers. 'The kid was asking Jason Woodford if he could hold his racket because it's *Jason*

Woodford. He didn't want to just hold any racket to see what it felt like.'

'Yeah, I know that now,' he says defensively.

'You really thought he would feel better holding anyone's racket?'

'I thought he might want to hold the racket of a star tennis player.'

'And you consider yourself a star tennis player.'

'You told me I have raw natural talent!' he cries, throwing his hands up in the air in exasperation. 'It's gone to my head.'

I stare at him, bewildered, before I tip my head back and burst out laughing. 'Oh my god, Harley!'

'I know.'

'You gave away your tennis racket.'

'I *know*.'

Still giggling, I shake my head at him, aghast. 'You're an idiot.'

'I know that, too.' He gives me a smile, picking up his drink. 'Thankfully, I have spares, but that was my favourite one. Although I used it today and we lost, so it's clearly not a lucky racket. Maybe it's not a bad thing to be rid of it.'

'Do you believe in that sort of thing?'

He takes a moment to consider his answer. 'I don't believe in lucky tennis rackets, but I think luck always has a part to play in life. Hard work only gets you so far. Sometimes you need a bit of luck to end up where you're supposed to be.'

'You think it was luck that delivered you to Wimbledon.'

'I've already said *that* was mostly down to you,' he corrects.

I smile modestly down into my drink. 'But a stroke of luck that Caleb injured himself and you stepped up to play that day Nick was deciding my new partner.'

'I'm not so sure about that.'

'It was bad luck, was it?'

'No, Dawson,' he says, his eyes locking with mine. 'I like to think that was fate.'

Oh god. Why does he have to say things like that? Things that make my stomach twist into knots. My cheeks growing hot, I quickly take another sip, averting my gaze and reminding myself that these are words. Good words, but words all the same, not actions. I've seen what he does when he thinks I'm not there.

I clear my throat pointedly, keen to change the subject and make things formal again.

Less . . . complicated.

'So,' I begin brightly, 'who do you think will be our biggest challengers next week? Aside from the Roehampton winners, obviously. And how do you think we can beat them?'

He straightens and, with a pensive expression, launches into his thoughts on the strongest players, while I nod along and do my best to stop myself from thinking about the kiss. And hating myself for wishing he would kiss me like that again.

*

We're silent in the lift going up to our hotel rooms.

I've purposefully stood on the opposite side of it to him, maintaining a safe distance. We ended up breaking Nick's rule and letting ourselves enjoy one more drink after the second round he bought us. If I'm honest with myself, it was a fun evening. Harley's so easy to talk to and, despite the elephant in the room that neither of us have addressed (the kiss), the conversation flowed and time flew. Before I knew it, it was getting dark and I forced myself to announce that we should get back.

His brow is furrowed as the lift climbs the floors. I imagine he's trying to work out how to broach the subject of what happened last night, maybe check to make sure that we're on the same page and I'm not under the misguided impression that it's anything more than what it was: a mistake.

We emerge onto our floor, still not saying anything as we make our way down the corridor until we're at my bedroom door. I get out my key, batting away that sense of déjà vu.

'Night, Harley,' I say breezily, making sure he knows that he doesn't have to worry – I'm not expecting anything. Not any more.

'Billie,' he says hurriedly, reaching out and brushing his hand against my arm.

I shiver at his touch, instinctively recoiling.

He frowns. 'I . . . I just wanted to thank you.'

'For what?'

He gestures down the corridor. 'For this whole Wimbledon experience.'

'We haven't even had the first day of the tournament yet,' I remind him, lifting my eyebrows. 'Technically, the experience hasn't started.'

'For me it has,' he says firmly, his brow furrowed in thought. 'The thing is, I've been wanting to say, in the last few weeks, things have become clearer for me. This sounds a bit out there, but I don't know how else to put it. The world feels that bit . . . brighter. Do you know what I mean? Sorry, I'm not saying it very well. Anyway, I think that's down to you.'

He runs a hand through his hair, leaving it even more dishevelled than usual. I remember how it felt to run my fingers through it last night and butterflies dance in my stomach. I try to ignore them.

'You mean, our fitness regime?' I say, swallowing the lump in my throat. 'Less drinking, early mornings, good workouts – your mind is clearer.'

He breaks into a smile, looking down at his shoes. 'Sure, that plays a part. But I mean . . . spending time with you.'

It's not fair. He's not allowed to say these things, not when I'm doing everything in my power to keep a level head. Did he say something similar to Grace Lewis this morning when he admired her necklace? Did he make her heart race with remarks about how her company made *his world feel brighter*? He's good at this. Well-practised.

'It's been fun,' I say briskly, bringing my protective barriers up, ready to deflect whatever charm he throws my way. 'Anyway, we should get some sleep.'

He doesn't move.

'Oh,' he says eventually, his shoulders slumping. 'Course.'

'See you tomorrow.'

'Yeah.'

I push open my door, step inside and, without looking back, I let it shut behind me.

CHAPTER TWENTY

All day, I have been regretting those three vodkas last night. If Harley or I were under any impression that Nick might go a bit gentler on us today after a long week, we were wrong. He reminded us that the Roehampton tournament was the beginning – this week coming is where the real work begins. We've been running drills, practising groundstrokes and going through our strategies so strictly that my brain aches as much as my muscles.

A hot bath alone in my hotel room is very welcome.

I've been lying here so long, the water is becoming lukewarm. Climbing out, I put on my fluffy robe and already regret not picking up some food on my way home. The idea of leaving this room to get some dinner is not tempting at all. All I want to do is crawl into bed, sink under my duvet and have someone bring me something to eat. For a moment, I pick up my phone and consider messaging Harley to ask if he can grab something for me – and then I remember that it's Saturday night and this is Harley Pierce I'm talking about. He won't be hiding away from London like I am; he'll be making the most of it.

'Plans tonight, Dawson?' he asked me earlier as we traipsed off the court.

'Oh, you know, big plans,' I replied breezily. 'Have a bath, watch TV, early night.'

'Wild.'

'What about you?'

'Oh, you know.' He shrugged, smiling at me. 'Big, wild plans, too.'

He didn't embellish and I didn't push for more detail. I'd rather not know.

He'll probably have taken a quick shower after our training and be out with one of the many girls he's met this week. Maybe Grace Lewis.

Refusing to let myself mope at the thought of who my tennis partner may or may not be pressing up against a hotel door tonight, I open the wardrobe to try to find something that I can throw on before I head out to the local supermarket.

There's a knock on my door.

It must be Nick coming to check on me. Hugging my robe closer round me, I plod over to my door and swing it open to find Harley on the other side. He's dressed up, wearing a smart pair of dark trousers and an olive-green linen shirt. He's styled his hair, and a faint waft of his cologne lingers in the air and is already making my legs feel weak.

He smiles at the sight of me. I remember that I've got my hair tied up in a messy bun on top of my head and no doubt my face is flushed from the bath.

Shit.

'Hey!' I say, startled by his appearance, my hand instinctively flying to my hair. Not that there's anything I can do right now to salvage the situation. 'What are you doing here?'

'We're heading out.'

My heart sinks. I glower at him, wondering why the hell he felt the need to disturb my evening to brag about his busy social life. 'Okay. Uh ... have fun?'

'Me and you, I mean.'

'What? Did Nick organize this? I thought he said we had the night to ourselves.'

'Nick hasn't organized anything,' he confirms, fiddling with the rolled-up sleeve of his shirt, his toned arms on display. 'I've organized this. If you want to get ready, I'd like to take you out for some dinner. And I promise to get you home in time for an early night.'

I stare at him, bewildered. 'You want to go for dinner.'

'That's right.'

'With me.'

'If you're not –' his eyes flicker down my robe and back up again – 'busy.'

'Is this another non-date?'

He slides his hands into his pockets. 'It can be whatever you want it to be, Dawson.'

Surprising myself, I find myself nodding. Maybe it's because he's all dressed up ready to go out and I would feel bad about turning him down when he's made an effort.

'Okay,' I say.

'I'll meet you downstairs in half an hour?'

'All right.'

With a satisfied smile, he turns and heads towards the lift, leaving me to shut the door and take a moment to work out what just happened. I'm not sure why I've agreed to this. There's no way that another evening with Harley is going to lessen my crush, no matter how much I remind myself that he's playing me as much as anyone else. I still can't help how I feel about him. He has a magnetic energy, a way of making everything... brighter. Just like he said last night.

I sigh, leaning against the door and burying my head in my hands, groaning through my fingers. I have got to keep it together. This is *not* a date. This is dinner with a friend. Lowering my hands, I smile to myself, biting my lip.

Of course, there's no harm in trying to make him *wish* it were a date.

I scurry across the room to the bed, picking up my phone and messaging Kat.

> **Billie**
> Remind me to thank you

> **Kat**
> For what?

> **Billie**
> For persuading me to pack that black dress

> **Kat**
> WHO IS THE LUCKY GUY?

When I walk out of the lift, Harley is waiting in the lobby. He glances up and does a double take. He jumps to his feet as I approach him in my fitted plunge-neck dress and heels. I breathe a stealthy sigh of relief, my body tingling with nerves. It's the reaction I was hoping for. I've taken a little longer than half an hour to get ready – I didn't want to rush my make-up, deciding that if I was going for this kind of dress, then I should complement it with a smoky eye and full lashes. I'm wearing statement gold earrings and have left my hair down in loose waves.

'Wow,' Harley breathes. His throat bobs as I stop in front of him. 'You look ... beautiful.'

'Thanks,' I say with a shy smile. 'So, where are we going? I may be overdressed.'

'You're perfect,' he says with a hint of tenderness that takes me by surprise and sends my heart jumping into my throat. 'Let's go.'

He moves to hold the hotel door open for me and I slide past him, waiting on the pavement while he hails a black cab. It doesn't take us long to reach Wimbledon Village, which is even busier tonight than it was yesterday, and I worry that he may have picked the worst place to go this weekend. I am swiftly proven wrong when we stroll into a smart restaurant on the high street to find a table waiting for us under Harley's name.

'Two glasses of champagne, please,' Harley says to the waiter as we take our seats.

I raise my eyebrows at him and he laughs.

'Come on, we're allowed one drink, and it may as well be a good one, especially when you're wearing that dress,' he argues with an impish grin. 'Let me be a little bit of a bad influence on you.'

'That's assuming you have any influence on me at all.'

'I can live in hope, Dawson.'

Tearing my eyes from his, I glance around the room, every table filled. 'Lucky you made a reservation. When did you book this?'

'A couple of nights ago.'

That would have been...

Thursday evening. That night flashes across my mind. The way he pulled me close to him. How I thought he'd bruise my lips he was kissing me so hard, but I didn't care – I only wanted more.

My face flushing, I grab my napkin to put it on my lap – anything to distract myself from looking at him.

'It's a nice place,' I say, trying to keep things vague and flat.

'Don't sound so surprised. I didn't do too badly with our first date, right?'

'You mean our first *non*-date. That's true. I still can't believe that was a jazz night. Such a great coincidence.'

'Actually, I have a confession about that.'

I glance up at him just as our drinks arrive. We wait for them to be placed down in front of us. When the waiter leaves, I follow Harley's lead and pick up my glass.

'Cheers,' he says, tapping his against mine.

'Hang on, what's this confession?' I ask, intrigued.

'At least let me have a quick drink before I make it,' he says, taking a sip of bubbles and then lowering his glass before taking a deep breath. 'That wasn't coincidence at all. I knew you listen to jazz. I picked that place on purpose because ... I hoped you would like it.' He pauses, dropping his gaze. 'I was trying to impress you.'

'But ... how did you know I like jazz?'

'Because I hear you play it in your room sometimes,' he explains with an apologetic expression. 'Not in a creepy way. I can't help it. In the summer, you have your window open and I have mine open and the music ... drifts.'

I stare at him in amazement.

He glances up at me. 'What?'

'Sorry, I . . .' I swallow. 'That was really thoughtful of you. '

'I'm glad you liked the bar.'

'I loved it.' I hesitate. 'Sorry that you've had to put up with my music – I had no idea. I'll turn it down.'

'Don't,' he says, smiling. 'You've been educating me.'

The waiter sidles over to the table to take our order and I hastily pick up the menu, but the words seem to blur across the page because my brain is swirling in a daze from this information. I'm picturing him thinking about where to take me, looking up various bars and pubs, searching for somewhere specific that he hoped I'd like. He didn't just take me anywhere. He took me somewhere he wanted me to like.

My heart swells.

Bet he does that with every girl, the smart bit of my brain responds.

I smile politely up at the waiter as I order my pasta dish. It takes all the effort I can muster to get through the meal with my guards still up. Every time Harley makes me laugh, I remind myself that everyone finds him funny. When my heart flips at his gorgeous smile, I think about Kat going on about how hot he is – that breathtaking smile isn't only for me. And when I catch him studying me in a way that sends flutters through my body, I recall Grace Lewis's sparkling eyes yesterday morning as she gazed up at him.

When I excuse myself at the end of the meal to go to the bathroom, I take a moment to look at my reflection in the mirror, breathing steadily, telling myself what I need to hear.

The kiss was a mistake.

It meant nothing to him.

It means nothing to me.

'We're here to play tennis,' I say out loud, opening my bag to refresh my lipstick.

Straightening, I sweep my hair behind my shoulder and give my reflection a quick, sharp nod. *We've got this*, I'm telling myself as I march back out, walls up, ready to face him again. But my fresh wave of fight is confronted the very moment I return to our table. Lying across the space where my plate had sat before it was cleared is a long, flat black box with swirling gold calligraphy etched into the top of it.

I slowly sit down, aware that Harley's eyes are fixed on me the whole time.

'What is this?' I ask.

'The reason I wanted to go out tonight,' he answers simply. 'I wanted time alone with you to give you this.'

I force myself to look up at him. 'You got me a gift?'

'I did.'

My fingers trembling a little, I carefully pick up the box and open the lid. My breath hitches. It's a delicate gold chain bracelet with a tennis racket charm.

'It's beautiful,' I whisper, my heart racing.

'It's from a local jewellery shop,' he tells me nervously. 'I got a recommendation from someone who grew up here – I wanted to get you something from Wimbledon while we're here, so I asked a junior player who would know the best place to—'

'Grace Lewis,' I stammer.

His eyebrows shoot up. 'Yeah. How did you know?'

I look up at him guiltily. 'I saw you talking to her yesterday morning. You swapped numbers. I thought . . .'

My sentence trails off as my eyes fall back down to the bracelet.

'Oh. *Oh*.' He places a hand on the table. 'Is that why you've been distant with me?'

I don't say anything, pressing my lips together.

'I wasn't giving her my number for *that*. I knew she was from Wimbledon, so I told her that I wanted to get you something special, and she was talking about how her boyfriend got her this necklace from a great little place in the Village. She needed my number so she could message me the name of it.' He pauses, his voice lowering and softening as he adds, 'Did you honestly think I'd have anyone else on my mind after that *kiss*?' A smile dances on his lips. 'No, Dawson. It's only you.'

My mouth is so dry, I have to swallow.

'I wanted to get you something from Wimbledon because I wanted you to have something that would always remind you of our time here,' he continues brazenly. 'No matter what happens, no matter where you are, I want you to be able to look at this charm on your wrist and know that someone out there believes that you, Billie Dawson, are capable of doing whatever the hell you want to do.' He pauses, waiting for me to bring my gaze up to meet his. 'That's me, by the way.'

Hot tears prick at the back of my eyes.

The kiss did mean something to him.

My heart is pounding so hard against my chest, I wouldn't be surprised if the whole restaurant can hear it, but I don't care. Everything around us has faded into a blur anyway. Suddenly, it's just me and him.

'Thank you,' I manage to say finally.

'You like it?' he asks, watching me, desperately trying to read my expression. 'If you don't, please say, because I can easy swap—'

'I love it, Harley.'

His shoulders drop with relief. 'Good. Here, let me help.'

He gestures for me to hold my hand out to him across the table, taking the bracelet from me to clasp it around my wrist. I bring my hand back to admire it.

'You really thought that I might be into Grace Lewis?' he says, dismayed.

I chew my lip. 'Yeah. I'm sorry. I totally misread that.'

'No, *I'm* sorry for letting you think … Billie, maybe I haven't been clear enough, and I don't want any more misunderstandings, so I'll just lay it all out for you. Okay, here goes.' He takes a deep, shaky breath, clearing his throat and leaning forward over the table to look me right in the eye. 'When I said to you last night that the world was brighter, I meant that you make my world brighter. I now know exactly what I want, and what I want is you. No one else.' He looks me in the eye and offers that playful smile of his, the one that makes my heart race. 'Dawson, if you're in, I'm in.'

Oh god. I can't breathe. I've actually stopped breathing.

He's staring at me expectantly, but I seem to have forgotten every word in the English language, my mouth parting but unable to make any sound. Suddenly, I understand what it means to be so shaken to your core that you don't trust yourself to speak.

In a good way.

Harley's eyes shift nervously around the other tables before coming back to me.

'Any time you want to say something, please go ahead,' he says, his forehead creased in concern. 'If that was too much, I get it, and I also understand if you're not on the same page. I promise that I'll keep things professional between us if you don't feel the same way – you don't need to worry about any awkwardness. I'll still play Wimbledon and we'll still be a great team . . . and I'm definitely rambling now but I can see that you're starting to smile so maybe I can –' he peers at me – 'hope?'

'You don't need to hope for anything, Harley.'

A flash of fear crosses his face, but if any lingers within him, I'm quick to obliterate it.

'You don't need to hope, because you should already know,' I tell him breathlessly, 'that I've been in since the moment you kissed me.'

'Only since then? Christ, Dawson, you have some catching up to do.' His eyes sparkle. 'I've been in since the moment I met the girl next door.'

CHAPTER TWENTY-ONE

Under the colourful hanging baskets of Wimbledon Village high street, Harley reaches for my hand, linking his fingers through mine and pulling me towards him. I smile as his other hand catches my waist before he dips his head to kiss me softly but surely, the busy street – the rest of the world – dimming in the background as I close my eyes and melt into him. Lifting my hands to cup his sculpted jaw, I kiss him back.

This is different to the hotel room. It's less urgent, every move and touch deliberate and savoured: the way his lips brush against mine, his hand freeing mine so it can drift round to the small of my back, gently pressing me against him, as his other holds me in place at the waist. When he parts my lips with his tongue to glide it against mine, my breath hitches and I thread my fingers through his hair, resting them at the nape of his neck as I arch my back, determined to be as close to him as possible. It's a warm evening, but I'm covered in goosebumps with the anticipation of tonight.

He draws back, a fierce intensity brightening his eyes.

'We should get back to the hotel,' I say in a raspy voice, my head still spinning from the kiss. I dig my teeth into my bottom lip and his breathing hastens.

'Yes, we should,' he says, kissing me again.

When we get into a taxi, he stays close, his warm leg pressing against mine. The skirt of my dress has hitched up as I sat down and he rests his hand on my thigh like it belongs there. As the car pulls away, Harley turns his head to face me and leans towards my ear, using his free hand to try to brush my hair out of the way. I get the hint, sweeping it back over the other shoulder so his lips are free to nip at my ear lobe, whispering, 'I can't wait to get you back to your room,' and sending a shudder through me. He smirks as I blush. He moves his attentive mouth to my neck, rolls of pleasure beginning to flutter through my body as his hand drifts higher up my thigh.

It's a short journey back to the hotel, but it feels like a torturously long time. He steps out of the taxi and holds his hand out for mine, helping me out before slamming the door shut. Locking our fingers together, both of us giggling, we make our way through the hotel doors and towards the lift. A couple of other guests step into the lift with us and we're forced to stand side by side without doing or saying anything, but the air is charged with tension. I'm dazzlingly aware of every move either of us makes, how he taps his hand impatiently against his leg, how shaky and uneven my breath is, how *good* his cologne smells standing this close. When his fingers brush against mine, a jolt of electricity shoots right through me.

When it gets to our floor, he takes my hand confidently in his and marches me to my room, spending the time it takes for me to fumble around my bag looking for the key card brushing my hair out of the way so he can kiss along my neck and shoulder, his hands roaming down the curve of my waist and along my hips.

As soon as we're through the door, I throw my bag onto the floor and spin round to face him, grabbing his head and pulling his lips to crash against mine. A low guttural sound comes from his throat as he grasps my hips to keep our balance, the kiss escalating into a frenzied urgency now that we're finally here alone and in private. I kick my shoes off and slide my hands down over his shoulders to fumble with the top buttons of his shirt, undoing them one by one until they're open enough to allow for my palms to press against his solid bare chest.

My desire for him erupts as his tongue becomes more rough and demanding and I moan into his mouth, a sound that causes him to lose all control. His hands drop and he lifts me up, my dress hitching up round the top of my thighs as my legs wrap instinctively round his waist, and he carries me to the bed, lowering me onto my back before pressing himself down on top of me. As I arch to grind my hips against his, I can feel he wants this as much as I do. He pauses, lifting himself to hover over me, the muscles of his arms flexing as he holds himself in place.

'Are you sure about this?' he asks hoarsely, his eyes searching mine.

'Yes,' I whisper, reaching for him, clawing for him, wanting to feel the weight of him on top of me again. I kiss him again, nipping at his bottom lip, adding, '*Yes*, I'm sure,' in case there's any doubt left in his mind.

Breaking into a relieved grin, he moves his lips along my jaw, down the slope of my neck, along my collarbone. I tip my head back, gasping for air as his fingers slide the straps of my dress down my arms. I lift up to help him draw the dress over my hips and down my legs. He finishes unbuttoning the rest of his shirt, taking it off and letting it drop to the floor. His eyes drift over me lying there in my underwear and as he moves to lean over me again, I bite my lip at the sight of him, my fingers digging into his arms as he sinks down on top of me.

I can't believe he's mine.

'You are so beautiful,' he's saying, his lips grazing against mine.

'I was just thinking the same about you,' I admit, smiling.

As he dips his head to kiss me deeply, I feel like I'm floating, like this is an impossible dream, one I can't bear to lose. Closing my eyes, I hold him tighter, knowing that, no matter what happens after tonight, it's too late for me now. I can pretend all I like, but the truth has become devastatingly clear.

Harley Pierce has my heart in his hands.

'I don't believe you,' I say with a giggle, turning on my pillow to look at Harley early the next morning as the sun streams in round the edges of the window blinds.

'It's true,' he insists, rolling on his side to face me properly, resting a hand on top of the sheet covering my stomach. 'I have always had the biggest crush on you. My mates have teased me about it for years, joking about me living next door to someone way out of my league and pining for you secretly.'

'If you've liked me for so long, how come you've never asked me out?'

He snorts. 'Uh, have you *met* you? I didn't have the guts. I never thought I'd be good enough.'

'That's ridiculous.'

'True, though. You'd have never said yes before now. That's why I had to play the long game,' he tells me proudly.

'What does that mean?'

'I had to bide my time, wrestle my way into your life and let *you* fall for *me*.'

I burst out laughing.

'It only took ten years, but here we are,' he adds, chuckling. 'I got you in the end.'

He reaches up to brush some strands of hair away from my

face, his fingers trailing along my cheekbone before he props himself up on his elbow to lean over and kiss me.

I'm still hardly daring to believe that we're here right now; that last night happened; that I fell asleep curled up safely in Harley's arms and woke this morning to find him next to me, our legs tangled together beneath the sheets, his arm holding me close to him as he slept. I thought I'd managed to creep to the bathroom without waking him, sorting myself out and making sure my appearance was acceptable before I emerged to find him waiting for me, smiling sleepily and gesturing for me to come back to him quickly.

I don't want this dream to end.

'I always thought you'd never look twice at someone like me,' I admit as he nestles his head back into his pillow, his hand resting on my hip as I roll on my side to face him.

He looks stunned. 'What, you thought beautiful, sexy girls weren't my type?'

'God, shut up.'

'It's *true*.'

I roll my eyes, fighting a bashful smile. 'I figured I was too boring in your eyes.' I hesitate. 'Which I probably am, to be honest.'

'That's not—'

'No, seriously. But things ... change.' I gaze over at him. 'Harley?'

'Mm?'

'You know how you said I made your world brighter?'

'I came up with that line all by myself, you know. Move aside, Shakespeare.'

I break into a wide smile. 'Since we've been working together, I've felt more ... open to things. Does that make sense?'

'You can say it, you know. I'll keep it between us. You don't need to worry – I promise I won't tell a soul and your fierce reputation will stay intact.'

'Say what?'

He looks at me intently. 'That I make your world brighter, too.'

I chew my lip. 'It's not my reputation I'm worried about.'

'Then what are you worried about?'

I swallow. 'How easy it is to lose someone,' I say quietly, my voice wavering.

His forehead creases. Then he edges closer to me, so our noses are almost touching. 'You won't be losing me, Dawson. My heart is the only one in danger of breaking here.'

His heart.

'Okay then,' I say, so softly, it's almost a whisper. 'You make my world brighter, too.'

He cups my face delicately in his hand. 'You see? The long game never fails. Ten years of pining, totally worth it.'

Then he leans forward to catch my laugh with his mouth.

CHAPTER TWENTY-TWO

Kat
Good luck today, Bills!
Sorry I missed your call yesterday
But I'll see you at the match today

Billie
Thanks so much!
That's okay
I listened to your voice note
You said you had some news?

Kat
It's okay
It can wait until later
You should be focused on Wimbledon!

> **Billie**
> Honestly, I'm so nervous
> I'd welcome a distraction
> Tell me!
> I feel like we haven't spoken properly in ages

Kat
Okay, so it's GOOD news
We may be seeing more of each other this summer!
I'm thinking I might go to to Europe another time
I might cancel my trip

> **Billie**
> Voice call
> *No answer*

> Voice call
> *No answer*

Kat
Sorry, I can't talk at the moment
I'm with Bards and I've got to leave him soon to come to London to cheer you on!

Billie

I just wanted to make sure you're ok???
Cancelling your Europe trip is a big deal!
You've wanted to do it forever!
You've been so excited about it?!

Kat

We can talk about it later
But of course I'm ok
I want this
I can do it any time
And this summer might not be the right one

Billie

Is that what Bards has told you?

Kat

Bills, I'm the one making this decision
I wish people would get that
Anyway, today is about YOU and Wimbledon!
I'm being anti-social so should probs go
But I love you and can't wait to see you xx

> **Billie**
> Voice call
> *No answer*

Junior Championships, Wimbledon 2025
Mixed Doubles First Round, Court 4
B. Dawson (GBR) & H. Pierce (GBR) vs
J. Bartos (CZE) & O. Benik (CZE)

The Monday of the second week of the Wimbledon Championships – and the official start to the Junior Championships – is a grey, cloudy day. Last week, we got lucky with the weather, but this week is looking less favourable, with rain forecast for tomorrow. But while the crowds of spectators might have been hoping for sun, I'm pleased it's overcast and cooler. Today has dragged on for ever. Ours is the final match of the day on this court and it's early evening by the time we step out onto Court Four to a smattering of applause from those who have stuck around long enough to watch the juniors play.

As I set my tennis bag down on the grass next to my chair to take out my things, I glance up to the seated stand to spot Jess, Tom, my dad and Kat, all sitting in a row, the boys sandwiched in the middle of my two best friends. Kat is wearing her sunglasses despite the dim light of the day, and I know she's not shielding her eyes so much as hiding them.

She's been crying today.

'Bards and her had a big fight last night,' Jess told me when I called her in a panic earlier after receiving Kat's message about cancelling Europe. 'He didn't get why she needed to spend all day today at Wimbledon when your match doesn't start until the evening. She did try explaining that you need to queue beforehand, but he didn't get it.'

'This is my fault,' I groaned. 'I wish I could have got you tickets so you didn't have to queue, but they only give us passes for family and coaches.'

'This is not your fault,' Jess said sternly. 'This is Bards being a jealous dickhead. You know why he's mad at her for coming to Wimbledon without him? Because she told him Tom was coming.'

'He's jealous of my brother?'

'Yeah, even though she's told him a million times that there's never been anything between them and it's not like she can avoid your family. But Bards made her feel like she was doing something wrong just by hanging out with another guy, even though he hangs out with other girls no problem. When I pointed that out to her, she got all uneasy and grumpy and ended up defending him.' Jess heaved a sigh. 'Now she's mad at *me* again.'

'She gets defensive when she knows you're right. She'll realize that soon and apologize – her stubbornness fades eventually.'

'I'm not sure.'

'Do you really think she might cancel Europe?'

'I don't know. What do we do?'

'I guess we have to trust she knows what she's doing.'

'And be there for her if things go wrong,' Jess added. 'How are you feeling about your match today? You and Harley on good terms?'

I bit back a smile. 'You could say that.'

'Oh my *god*, I know that tone! You slept together, didn't you?'

I gasped. 'How the HELL could you tell that from my voice?!'

'Ahhh!' she screeched, before bursting out laughing. 'I couldn't tell, but you've just confirmed it for me! DETAILS NOW.'

I was happy to oblige and it was a good conversation that distracted me from the all-consuming nerves flooding my veins at the thought of this match. We beat Bartos and Benik at Roehampton, but that's no guarantee that we'll have the same result today. That's the beauty of Wimbledon – you never know what might happen.

You can feel the proud heritage of Wimbledon the moment you walk through the gates, your hands tingling at the thought of the number of champions who have stepped into this club hoping to make history. The air is filled with excitement, hope, crushing disappointment. It's an honour to be playing on the grass courts of Wimbledon, especially as a Brit, even a junior one. Nothing beats playing in front of a home crowd. That's what Nick reminded me earlier on the practice courts: 'Feel the pleasure of playing here at Wimbledon; forget everything else. Enjoy it, however it goes.'

I unzip my jacket, fold it and crouch down to place it in my tennis bag before pulling out my racket. As I straighten, Harley leans towards me to say in a low growling voice, 'So. Come here often?'

I break into a smile. 'You're an idiot.'

'By the way, I signed us up for a tap-dance competition in October,' he says brightly. 'I figured once this is over, we'd want something else to work towards.'

'Please tell me you're joking.'

'Nope! Are you excited? I am.'

'No, I am not excited!' I hiss through gritted teeth. 'You have got to stop signing me up for things without my permission.'

'I know you don't mean that and you're secretly as excited as I am.' Glancing round us, he leans closer to whisper, 'Also, do you know how sexy you look when you're mad? I'm excited to fight with you. Then make up. Then fight again.'

'Harley, this is really not the time to—'

'Let's do this!' he cries, beaming at the spectators in the stand, giving our support crew a cheery wave.

Rolling my eyes at his back, I can't help but laugh, the

tension that's been weighing down on me all day lifting a little. He has a knack at doing that.

As he jogs onto the court to begin our warm-up – and I hear Jess's, 'Whoop!' – it strikes me that no one has shown up for Harley today. He has Nick, but he's our coach – he *has* to be here. And sure, my dad, Tom, Jess and Kat are cheering for both of us, but they're my family and friends. Bards could have joined Kat today easily if he'd wanted, saving himself an argument with his girlfriend and, at the same time, being there for a big moment in his friend's life. He obviously really didn't want to come. And neither of Harley's parents are in the crowd today. In fact, he hasn't mentioned that they'd be coming at all this week, even if we kept making it through to the next round.

I glance over at Harley as he jokes with the ball boy, who is chucking him options to practise his serves with. He catches my eye and smiles, a surge of flutters filling my chest as I smile back at him. I decide then and there to be Harley's support crew from now on.

I hope he knows that I plan on always showing up for him.

We're one set up – six games to four – and we're currently five games to three in the second set. The score of this game stands at fifteen–thirty, and it's Benik serving.

Things got off to a rocky start when Bartos and Benik won the coin toss and chose to serve first, winning the first game of the match in straight points. My nerves had got the better of me, but as we changed ends after the first game and Harley prepared to serve, he whispered, 'If my first serve is an ace, you're buying me dinner tonight.'

I shot him a look that said: *This is Wimbledon; stop messing around.* But I'm not sure he got all that from my warning glare because he sauntered up to the service line, and as the court descended into a nerve-racking silence, he tossed the ball up and served an ace so brilliant and fast, I gasped and our opponents looked like they had no idea what hit them. Harley came jogging over to tap my hand, saying, 'Sweet. Just so you know, I'll be ordering lobster,' before heading back to the baseline.

His attitude has rubbed off on me, lifting my spirits, and when we broke their serve during the first set, I knew then that we were going to win it. Now, all we need to do is break them again and we've won the match.

Fifteen–thirty.

Two points. That's all we need. *Two points.*

Taking a deep breath, I ready myself on the balls of my feet for Benik's serve. Selecting his ball and passing the others back to the ball girl behind him, he wipes the sweat off his brow with his wristband before peering down our end of the court.

It's always a strange moment, the one just before the serve. Everything slows and stills until it feels like time has stopped.

The silence on the court is almost unbearable. I can hear my heart pounding, my long exhale wavering.

Then as soon as the strings of the racket hit the ball, the court springs into life.

Benik's serve is precise and quick, coming across my body. I lunge to get my racket behind it, slicing it slowly back across to Benik, who has time to plan where to place it next. Harley starts to retreat to join me at the baseline. Benik sees this and gently slices the ball short. It drops our side of the net where Harley was positioned moments ago . . . But Harley is back there in a flash, having baited the drop shot. Benik fell into his trap. With a flick of his wrist, Harley places the ball at an impossible angle across the court, inches from the net. Bartos has no chance, lowering her racket as the ball zips past her, knocking over a water bottle by the umpire's chair.

'Fifteen–forty,' the umpire announces.

As the stand cheers, I'm grinning like a bobcat, reminding myself to tell Harley when this is over how much I admire the way he does shots like that. His tennis style is almost an extension of his character – playful, unpredictable, fun. Nick has told me before that while power is good, sometimes I could take a leaf out of Harley's book and go with the unexpected mischievous shots. I only wish I had the courage.

I move up to the net, crouching as we await Benik's serve.

Bringing his racket up over his shoulder to meet the ball, he roars with the effort and a blur of yellow soars past me. It's so good, I know it won't be returned.

'Thirty–forty.'

There's disappointment etched across Harley's forehead as we pass each other, but I say, 'We've got this,' as our hands touch, convincing myself as much as him. Waiting for Benik to select the ball for his serve, I tighten my ponytail and inhale deeply. Dad is watching. On Friday, he watched me lose at Roehampton.

But on this point, I will be a winner.

'We will be winners,' I mutter under my breath as Benik steps up to serve, thinking that maybe saying it out loud will help my case.

The ball goes up in the air . . . Benik swings at it . . .

. . . it smashes into the net.

'Second serve, Benik,' the umpire tells us.

I roll my neck, shake out my ankles and crouch again, ready for his second serve. It goes in and I step towards it, rocketing it back cross-court to Benik. I sprint to the net, hoping to put pressure on our opponents by standing side by side with Harley. Benik has one option: a lob. He pushes the ball up and over both of us. It's a great ball, and as I watch it go up, Harley's voice creeps into my brain: *You go for every shot.*

Fuck yes, I do.

I've spun round and am racing back to greet Benik's lob as it lands just two feet from the baseline. It bounces and, facing the back of the court, I awkwardly swing my racket across my body, hitting the ball under my left arm. I hear the gasps of the spectators at such an attempt – it's messy, but it works. I stumble forward and quickly look back to see the ball returning high over their side of the court.

Uh oh.

Benik looks relaxed as the ball drops to where he's waiting for it, his arm raised to smash it back. He hits it hard and fast – the ball makes a loud *crack* as it skims the top of the net, which takes the speed off. It's thrown up and over to us. Harley is there.

He returns a perfect slice drop shot that almost bounces backwards when it lands inches from our opponents' side of the net.

'Game, set, match, Dawson and Pierce,' the umpire declares.

Harley punches the air. We're through to the second round.

The first person up on their feet in the stand is my dad. I grin at him, my eyes scanning along Jess's and Tom's ecstatic expressions as they cheer louder than everyone else.

That's when I notice Kat is no longer there. I have no idea when she left.

CHAPTER TWENTY-THREE

Tom is the only one waiting for me when I emerge into the fresh air from the changing rooms. His face lights up, throwing his arms open to pull me into a giant hug before drawing back to give me a playful punch on the arm.

'Yes, Bills!' he cries, beaming at me. 'That was incredible! Second round, bring it on. Proud of you.'

'Thanks,' I say with a smile. 'How are you? How are you feeling? You should get home soon so you can rest; it's been a busy day and—'

'Christ, Bills, you've just won a junior match at *Wimbledon*,' he says, looking at me wide-eyed in disbelief. 'It's a big deal. So do you think you could, I don't know, enjoy the moment a little? Stop worrying about anything and everything for five minutes?'

'I'm not worrying about *everything*,' I correct, smiling with amusement at his teasing. 'I'm worrying about you. You're still not completely recovered.'

'I'm fine. In fact, I'm better than fine. I'm ecstatic!' He reaches out to grip my shoulders. 'My sister just got through the first round of her tournament!'

I laugh giddily, glancing around. 'Where's everyone else?'

'Well, Harley came out a few minutes ago and he decided to accompany Dad and Jess to the gift shop. Get this: the gift shop was Dad's idea.'

I give him a strange look. 'Really?'

'Yep, he said he needed to get something real quick. Weird, right? Come on.' He throws his arm round my shoulders, dragging me in that direction. 'I said I'd wait for you and then we'd go and meet them there. So, how does it feel?'

'Good. A relief.' I exhale the air from my cheeks. 'Terrifying.'

'All the right things to feel after a win like that one,' he comments, squeezing me close and grinning as he drops his arm to his side. 'The adrenaline is working its magic.'

'How about you?'

'I told you, I'm fine! I'm having, like, a weird proud twin moment. I want to shout it to everyone. In fact, I might do just that.' He waves at a couple passing by, before pointing to me and going, 'My twin sister just won a match in the juniors tournament!'

'Congratulations,' they say in chorus, smiling warmly at me.

Blushing with embarrassment and muttering my thanks, I glare at him as he cackles with laughter.

'What? I'm allowed to show you off,' he proclaims, delighted with himself. 'And you should make the most of this moment.'

'Because it may not last?'

'Because it's a *big achievement*.' He rolls his eyes. 'Jeez.'

I chuckle. 'Sorry. You're right. Thanks.'

Studying his gleeful expression as we stroll through the crowd, I purposefully slow when we get nearer to the giftshop until I'm at a standstill. I turn to face him.

'Tom, can I ask you something?'

'If you're going to ask for notes, then I don't have any.'

'No, I'm all good for notes, thank you – I have Nick,' I remind him with a wry smile. 'I wanted to ask if you were okay about being here at Wimbledon, watching me play.'

He visibly balks. 'What? That's a stupid question.'

'No it's not,' I say gently, looking guiltily down at the ground. 'I've been so wrapped up in everything that's going on with me and focusing on the match, I didn't stop to think about how it might feel for you to watch this knowing you should be playing alongside me.'

His expression softens. 'Bills, I don't care about that.'

'Because I really do miss playing with you and if I'd had it my way—'

'Yeah, I know,' he says, holding up his hands, 'we'd have been playing together like you always planned it. But you can't plan much in life, can you. That's what I'm starting to realize, anyway. That is actually a good thing.'

'It is?'

He nods slowly. 'Sometimes you need a spanner to throw you off course and make you realize what else is out there, and what else you can do or be. If you're too focused on achieving one single goal, you might miss out on all the fun. I like the idea of taking my hands off the steering wheel every once in a while to see where life takes me. Maybe you should do the same.'

'Have you been spending your time off reading self-help books or something?' I ask, raising my eyebrows at him. 'You sound like Oprah.'

'That's a massive compliment.' He laughs, placing a hand on my shoulder. 'My point is, I don't want you to think that I'm sitting there watching you with any kind of regret or resentment, or wishing I was playing with you, because I'm not.'

'You mean you don't miss the nerves that make you feel sick or the crushing pressure? Huh.'

'Weirdly, no,' he says, as we share a knowing smile. He hesitates. 'Don't tell anyone I said this, but the only thing I miss is spending all that time with you.'

'Aw.' I jab my finger in his shoulder. 'You are so *adorable*. You miss your sister.'

He lifts his eyes to the sky. 'Don't go overboard.'

'You're a big softie at heart, aren't you, you little cutie-pie. You *miss* me.'

'You are the worst.'

'Don't worry, I won't tell a soul about how much you miss me,' I say, reaching out in an attempt to squish his cheeks.

'I take it back; I don't miss you at all,' he grumbles, batting away my hands. He notices something, reaching out to lift my wrist. 'This a new bracelet? Looks expensive.'

I pull my hand away, feeling myself blush. He looks at me intrigued.

'Hey! There you are!' Jess calls out, bounding up to us at just the right moment and throwing her arms around my neck. 'You were amazing! Honestly, Billie, I've never seen you play like that before.'

She draws back to stare at me in wide-eyed wonder.

'Thanks so much for coming; it means so much to have you here,' I say, pulling her back into a hug and holding her tight.

'Of course!' She laughs as I let her go. 'I've already asked Tom if I can join him and your dad tomorrow.' She gestures around us. 'Wimbledon is so much fun, by the way. I'm a fan for life.'

'It's pretty great, right? Where's Kat?'

Her smile falters. 'Uh ... she had to go home early. She left after the first set.'

I try not to look too disappointed. 'Oh! She didn't see the win?'

Jess shakes her head. 'But she was so proud of you that first set. I know how sad she'll be to have missed the rest.'

'She had to head home to Bards,' Tom tells me wearily. 'The whole time you were playing, he was messaging her. It was making her pretty upset.'

Jess sighs. 'Whatever. Please can we not talk about that guy when you've had such a big win today. I know he's Harley's mate, but –' she glances around before lowering her voice – 'I *really* don't like him.'

'I'm not sure I'm his biggest fan, either,' I comment, before spotting Harley and my dad over her shoulder emerging from the gift shop.

I can't stop myself from lighting up at the sight of Harley, who is deep in conversation with my dad as they stroll towards us together. Dad is carrying a bag from the gift shop and Harley is nodding along to whatever he's saying. Harley then makes a remark and Dad tips back his head to laugh. I glance to Tom and he shoots me a knowing smile.

'Your new tennis partner is making a good impression,' he notes.

'Yes, I hear he's a great smash off the court as well as on it,' Jess says, winking at me.

I glare at her. Alarmed by Jess's comment, Tom glances from her to me and back to her again before he goes, 'Oh god, *bleugh*. Really, Jess? Was that necessary?'

'Just saying what I've heard, Tom,' she replies innocently.

'*Jess*,' I hiss, before plastering on a big smile as the two of them reach us.

'Billie,' Dad says, drawing me into a hug, which is a gesture that doesn't come that naturally to him, so it's a bit awkward for both of us, 'you were *fantastic*.'

'Really?' I step back to look at him properly. 'Do you think so?'

'Yes. Actually, I was saying to Harley that I think I might owe you ... an apology.'

Dad's eyes fall to the ground.

Tom clears his throat. 'Does anyone want to get some strawberries?'

'Yes!' Jess squeaks, getting the message loud and clear.

'I do.' Harley nods vigorously.

'Great! We'll come find you two in a bit,' Tom says to me and Dad, before the three of them turn and disappear into the late evening crowd.

Dad waits for them to go and then takes a deep breath. 'Yes, as I was saying, I want to apologize. I haven't been paying attention to your progress. Not really. I've always known you were good – better than good – but, my god.' He hesitates. 'Billie, you were magical out there today.'

I force myself to look up and find him watching me with glistening eyes.

'When I saw you play last Friday, I was stunned at how good you were,' he says a little croakily. 'It was like you were a different person on the court, and I felt so ashamed that I had no idea just how brilliant you are. I wanted to tell you that in person, which is why I've waited until today – I'm sorry I couldn't hang around after that match.'

'I lost on Friday,' I remind him quietly.

'It doesn't matter – you were still *stunning* to watch,' he asserts, throwing me with the firmness in his tone. 'You're never going to win every match, Billie, even the best players in the world know that. But you learn from each and every point, and look at you today – you have already grown as a player over just one weekend.'

I smile up at him. 'Harley had a lot to do with it.'

'He's a very strong player and he suits you. I can see why Nick pushed for the pairing.' He gives me a look. 'There is more you could both be doing, and I've made some notes if you'd care to hear them.'

'I would,' I say, swallowing the lump in my throat.

No one but Tom would understand how much it means for my dad to have made notes on my game. For someone else, it might seem patronizing or boring or strange. But for me, it means he's finally taking me seriously. *He thinks I can do it.*

'Good. I hope you don't mind, but I also studied some of your opponents over the weekend and I might have some pointers there. I'm sure Nick has already got it covered, but you never know – it's always helpful to share notes.'

'Thanks, Dad.'

'Let's go back to the hotel and we can run through it all,' he says excitedly.

'Okay,' I say, dazed by this surreal conversation. 'Sounds like a plan.'

'Oh, before we go –' he reaches into the Wimbledon gift-shop bag and lifts out a giant tennis ball, handing it to me – 'here.'

'Uh ... thanks?' I say, tucking it under my arm. 'I don't have one of these.'

'That's not for you,' he says, reaching into the inside of his jacket pocket and pulling out a pen. He holds it out for me to take. 'It's for me. I would like you to sign it.'

I stare at him. 'What?'

'I would like you to sign that for me,' he says, puffing out his chest. 'I'm going to put it on the mantelpiece, pride of place. My daughter, a Junior Wimbledon champion.'

'But ... I'm only through to the second round. I haven't won anything.'

'That's not how I see it,' he adds, pressing the pen into the palm of my hand.

Unable to trust myself to say anything thanks to the lump stuck in my throat, I pull the lid off the pen and start scrawling my signature across the neon-yellow tennis fluff of the iconic giant Wimbledon ball, while my dad watches on silently, a proud smile on his face.

CHAPTER TWENTY-FOUR

> **Kat**
> I'm so sorry I missed the end of your match, Bills

> I PROMISE I'll make it up to you
> Somehow xxx

I know it's incredibly frustrating for everyone involved – players, spectators, organizers – but it wouldn't be right for there to be no rain days at all throughout the Wimbledon fortnight. It has to happen, and this year it happens on Tuesday, so our next round is delayed until Wednesday.

I do everything possible not to let the extension of time in the lead-up cause the building nerves to overwhelm me. Harley and I go for a run first thing on Tuesday morning, laughing and trying to beat the other one's time, stealing kisses in the early drizzle. We run drills and train with Nick on indoor practice courts, and during the downtime in the late afternoon, I don't sit around and let myself worry about tomorrow – I go for a swim and spend time in the sauna. I messaged Harley to invite him to join me there, but he didn't reply for a while, and by the time he did, I'd already left to go back to my room.

In the evening, Harley and I join Nick for a chilled dinner in a restaurant nearby, and before Harley has even sat down I can tell something is off. His expression is stony and serious, his forehead creased, his mouth in a hard, straight line.

'You okay?' I ask, smiling at him as he takes his seat next to me.

'Fine,' he mumbles through a fixed smile before he disappears into himself again.

He barely says a word the whole time, listening to Nick as he runs through our strategies and the opponents' weaknesses one more time, but not joking or teasing like he usually does. I'm so used to being the tense one while Harley does well to relax me or put me at ease that I'm thrown by the switch in our roles, but I'm determined to help him feel better.

'Hey,' I say gently, reaching out to take his hand when Nick goes to the bathroom and we have a moment to ourselves, 'we're going to be okay tomorrow. It's good to be nervous.'

'Yeah, I know,' he says, barely looking at me.

He squeezes my hand but drops it long before he needs to – Nick hasn't reappeared, yet. I watch him curiously, wondering if there's more to this than the looming second round, but when we go upstairs in the hotel, he waits for Nick to shut his bedroom door before he quickly slides into my room, sweeping me into his arms and kissing me like he's been holding out for ever, urgently, roughly, desperately. I sigh with relief against his lips because I need him too, a heavy ache filling my stomach as he holds me in place pressed up against him, his hands grasping my hips, my nails digging into his shoulders.

When he breaks the kiss, he lifts his head, his hands moving up to cup my face. Breathing heavily, he studies me as though checking I'm really there and not a figment of his imagination. I can tell something is troubling him still, his dark eyes glistening with an uncertainty and apprehension that wasn't there before.

'I'm so lucky to have you,' he rasps.

I place a hand over his, grasping his fingers, doing my best to give him a reassuring smile. 'You're not going to lose me. I need you,' I say, because somehow I feel that's what he needs to hear right now. This wonderful, caring, vulnerable guy, who is ignored by his parents and underestimated by everyone else. Once underestimated by me.

I need him.

He exhales a long breath, his shoulders visibly relaxing before he pulls me into a hug, burying his face in my hair and neck, wrapping his strong arms around my waist and holding me close. I press my lips against his ear, kissing him softly.

'We'll be okay,' I reassure him. 'This is just pre-match nerves.'

I can hear him swallow. He releases me, stepping back and inhaling deeply through his nose. He attempts a smile, giving me a nod.

'Yeah, course,' he says, his voice a little strained. 'Everything will be okay.'

'See you in the morning?' I say regretfully but sensibly – we both agreed on Sunday that sleep this week was of utmost importance, and if we're in the same bed, it would be much harder to get much of that.

'See you in the morning,' he confirms, kissing me lightly and turning to leave.

I move to stand in the doorway, watching him make his way down the empty corridor to his room, his hands in his pockets, his head bowed. I close the door, suppressing a gut instinct that something isn't right.

'Just pre-match nerves,' I repeat in a whisper to myself.

But I feel as unconvinced as Harley looked when I told him the same.

Junior Championships, Wimbledon 2025
Mixed Doubles Second Round, Court 6
B. Dawson (GBR) & H. Pierce (GBR) vs
K. Ryan (AUS) & L. Marino (ITA)

We're down four games to five in the first set, and with the score currently at thirty–forty in Harley's service game, it's break point for Ryan and Marino.

Harley is distracted.

He's made some basic unforced errors and his head isn't in the game, I can tell. Nick can tell, too – he's leaning forward on the edge of his seat in the front row by the side of the court, his eyebrows knitted together. I regret not encouraging Harley to talk to me more last night, and guilt is rolling through my belly as I crouch in preparation.

He was fine yesterday morning, but by dinner he wasn't himself. I'd assumed it was to do with the tournament because I wanted it to be that; it was easier to make it be that. Nothing to do with his family or his friends. *Nothing to do with me.*

I hear Harley bounce the ball on the line and the faint *whoosh* of the toss, but the serve never comes, and I can tell from the way Ryan straightens and then repositions herself as she prepares to return that Harley didn't get the toss right first. She crouches lower and I hear Harley try again, this time striking the ball straight into the net.

'Second serve, Pierce,' the umpire utters.

Harley does a slice serve into Ryan's body, who has stepped in closer to receive it. She jolts sideways to create some space for her swing, returning it flat across to Harley. He plays it back cross-court and she sends it to him again. This goes on for several shots, neither wanting to make a mistake. Harley is playing it safe. I'm at the net waiting to pounce, edging closer to the centre to either try to bait a shot down the tramline or steal a cross-court return to end this point.

Ryan finally makes a good enough error for me to take advantage of, hitting her return close to me. I punch the ball hard past Marino, who doesn't react quick enough. Ryan sprints across the baseline to cover him, diving forward and just getting her racket behind the ball.

It soars high up into the air over my head.

Harley is waiting beneath it as it descends. His racket is back and up, ready to meet the ball. *Smack*. The ball sails past me, past Ryan, past their baseline, hitting the backboard of the court.

'Out,' roars a line judge as though that wasn't obvious.

'Game. First set, Ryan and Marino,' the chair umpire informs the crowd.

I watch Harley put his hands on his hips, hanging his head in frustration.

As we take our seats at the side of the court, I know that we don't have much time – definitely not enough to talk about anything properly. I think about how he has always used his humour and storytelling skills to lift me up during a match when I need it, and I realize that it's my turn to be what he needs right now: a cheerleader.

After swigging from my water bottle and dabbing at my

face with my towel, I lean towards him and say in a low voice, 'You know what I love about tennis?'

He looks at me glumly. 'Winning?'

'That's part of it, sure – you know how competitive I am – but that's not the main reason. No, what I really love about tennis is how the moment you step out on the court, you get to take back control.'

His brow furrows as he listens.

'No matter what's going on in your life, how you feel about anything else, whatever is hurting you – here on this grass, you're no longer powerless,' I tell him, lifting my chin, gazing out across the court. 'Everything else around you can be chaos, but not here in this space. This is a level playing field. Here you can take control.'

He's watching me carefully. 'But whoever you're playing can steal that from you.'

'And you have equal opportunity to steal it back.'

That prompts a small smile from him, enough to give me a boost of confidence to carry on with the next part of my little pep talk.

'You know what else I love about tennis? It's fucking *fun*,' I say, grinning and giving his knee a small nudge with mine. 'I'd forgotten that, I think, until I started playing with you.'

'Tom was that boring, huh?'

'Look, my brother is great, but has he ever attempted and failed at doing a randomly cute little frog leap in between rallies like you did a couple of weeks ago? No. Years we've played together, and he's never provided that level of entertainment.'

'I wasn't doing a *frog leap*,' he says defensively. 'I was breakdancing to celebrate that amazing drop shot Nick never saw coming.'

'Hey, call it what you will – it was fascinating.'

Harley laughs, shaking his head.

'Tell you what, let's make this interesting,' I say, straightening with excitement at the genius of the idea that's just cropped up into my mind. 'If we win this match, I'll give it a go.'

'Give what a go?'

'Your frog leap.'

'*Breakdancing.*'

'Whatever.'

He looks at me, licking his bottom lip. 'You're serious?'

'Deadly. If we lose, you can do it.'

Harley glances around at the spectators. 'You're saying that if we win, you will do some breakdancing on this court in front of all these people, who all own camera phones.'

'A bet is a bet. I won't back down from it. And we both know you won't.'

'Time,' the umpire announces.

I quickly hold out my hand. 'We got a deal?'

Looking at me in disbelief, Harley takes my hand and shakes it. 'Deal.'

We return to the court and, no matter how this plays out, I feel like I've achieved something in the way Harley is still grinning as he makes his way over to the baseline. I spin my racket around in my grip, feeling lighter somehow.

That feeling of contentment only grows into joy as the second set begins, with Harley back on top form, playing like he's suddenly remembered he can win. That happiness surges when we win the second set six games to three. And it erupts when we win the ten-point tie-breaker that's in lieu of a third set. We're through to the quarter-finals.

I'm not sure the win is worth the humiliation of a very public, completely ridiculous, utterly random celebratory frog leap on Court Six of Wimbledon.

But the way Harley roars with laughter is.

CHAPTER TWENTY-FIVE

Harley and I are on such a high when we get back to the hotel that we don't notice Kat and Bards at first. Harley is cackling with laughter as we relive my frog-leap, throwing his arm around my shoulders and drawing me close to him.

'I still can't believe you did that!'

'A bet is a bet,' I maintain, grinning wildly as we walk through the door.

'Maybe we need to sign up to breakdancing lessons this summer as well as our—'

He stops dead in his tracks in the middle of the hotel lobby, his eyes growing wide with shock. I follow his eyeline to see Bards and Kat jumping up from the sofa there. Bards is smiling at us, throwing his arms out, a bottle of whisky in his hand. The hotel receptionist is eyeing him up warily.

'Surprise!' he calls out, swaggering over to Harley as Kat comes rushing at me.

I envelop her in a huge hug and she holds on a little longer than usual.

'What are you doing here?' I ask as she draws back to beam at me.

'It was Bards's idea,' she gushes. 'This afternoon we were at the pub and I was saying how bad I felt about missing your match the other day, so he said we should hop on a train and surprise you at your hotel!'

'Why not, eh?' Bards says, nudging Harley, who gives a small, uneasy smile. I can smell the alcohol on Bards's breath from here. 'So, come on then – did you win? Are we celebrating or commiserating?'

'We won,' I tell him, prompting Kat to cheer and clap her hands.

'Lucky I brought the hard stuff, then!' he exclaims, shaking the bottle before he lowers it along with his voice, his eyes shifting towards the receptionist. 'Although I probably shouldn't draw too much attention to bringing my own booze. You want to crack this open in your room or go to the bar for an appetizer?'

'Bards, it's really ... nice of you both to make the effort to come all this way and surprise us,' Harley begins, his eyebrows knitted together, 'but we can't drink.'

'What? You're having us on, right?' Bards chuckles, slapping him on the back.

'We're playing tomorrow in the quarter-finals,' Harley says

firmly. 'It's important. We can't drink the night before and we really need to get to bed.'

'Oh. Right.' Bards's jaw tightens and his eyes flicker to me. 'I hear you. You two need to *get to bed*. What happened to bros before hoes, huh?'

'I didn't mean—' Harley starts quietly, but Kat cuts in, sensing the tension and placing a hand on Bards's arm.

'They need an early night, Bards – they have a big match tomorrow,' she says, as Bards sniffs in disapproval. 'We just hoped you might be able to come for one drink at least.'

'Yeah,' Bards says, lifting his chin as he stares hard at Harley as though challenging him to give another excuse. 'One can't hurt, right? *Mate?*'

Harley glances at me.

'What, you need the missus to give you permission or something?' Bards says, not bothering to hide his irritation. 'Can't think for yourself any more – that it?'

'*Bards*,' Kat says in a strained voice, her expression twisting with worry.

'What? We've come all this way to surprise them and they're telling us to go,' he says with a shrug, gesturing to me. 'Things change, I guess.'

'Nothing's changed,' Harley says, pained.

I want to rip Kat away from Bards and tell him to fuck right off, but I also hate seeing Harley so torn, desperately wanting to do the right thing, but finding it difficult to disappoint his friend. So, I jump in to help him out.

'We can have one drink,' I say brightly, my eyes fixed on Bards as he turns to look at me in surprise. 'You have come all this way.'

'Hey, there you go,' he says. 'Glad someone is making sense. Let's go to the bar.'

'Thanks, Bills,' Kat says with a smile, squeezing my arm before she and Bards lead the way.

'Billie,' Harley says urgently hanging back with me, 'I don't want to drink. It won't be just one; he'll keep them coming and—'

'Harley, you don't have to do everything he says,' I point out, finding his hand as we follow them. 'When we're done, we say we're done. They can carry on if they like.'

He exhales a deep breath. 'He can be very persuasive. Look, he's a different person when he's had a few, all right? That impression you have of him is probably not going to get any better.'

'It's okay, stop worrying,' I assure him. 'Considering Kat has fallen for his charm and you're his best friend, there must be something about him.'

Harley's frown deepens.

'Harley, what is it?' I ask, stopping him and glancing over at Bards. 'What are you not telling me? Has he got something to do with you being distracted earlier?'

Visibly pained, his eyes fall to the floor. 'I . . . I can't go into it now. It's a bit of a nightmare for the two of them to have shown up here. Last thing I fucking need.'

'It will be fine. I'm here with you, remember? Whatever it is that's going on between you and Bards, I'm sure you can work it out. And don't worry, I'll make sure there's no alcohol in our drinks.'

'How are you going to do that?'

I shoot him a knowing smile. 'Leave it with me.' I clear my throat, leaning on the bar next to Bards, who has the bottle of whisky tucked under his arm. 'My round, Bards. No arguments. Least I can do since you've travelled here.'

'Classy,' he says, grinning at me. 'All right, thank you, Ice Princess.'

I pretend not to be unnerved by the way his eyes flicker down to my chest and back up again. As Kat's friend, I'm trying really hard to like her boyfriend, but he's not making it easy.

'Gin and tonic?' I suggest.

'A double,' he states. 'With a couple of slices of cucumber.'

'Coming right up.'

Giving me a nod, he struts away from the bar to join the table that Kat and Harley have chosen. Looking over my shoulder at them, I can see that the conversation isn't exactly flowing. Harley looks like he's doing his best to avoid her eye contact or talk to Kat at all, pretending to be interested in his surroundings of the bar.

'Your friend can't drink that in here,' the barman says sternly, grabbing my attention. I spin back to face him. 'The one with the whisky bottle.'

'I know. He ... bought that as a gift. We won't drink it now. If he does, feel free to kick him out. You might be doing me a favour.'

'Fair enough. What can I get you?'

'Two double gin and tonics, and then two glasses of tonic water. But can you put cucumber in all of them so the tonic water looks like it's got alcohol in it?'

He smiles in understanding.

By the time I bring the drinks over to our table, Bards is in the middle of telling a funny sports-day story about him and Harley at school, and I join in with Kat's giggles, wary of Bards but also eager to hear more about Harley, who is smiling bashfully at his feet. We bring our glasses together to cheers and Bards continues, the star of the show and centre of attention, playing up for our laughs.

There's no question he's an animated storyteller, and as the conversation flows, I start to understand more of his appeal: he's fun, lively, engaging. If Harley wasn't acting so awkwardly around him, I'd be more open to trying to like him for his sake as well as Kat's, but it's obvious from Harley's body language andlacklustre conversation that they've had a fallout – anyone would be able to tell that Harley is holding some kind of grudge right now. I have no idea what it could be about, but until I know, I'm automatically on his side.

We may have got away with the first round, but Bards orders more drinks – Harley and I don't touch ours, but Bards doesn't seem to notice. He swigs away at his, Kat continually glancing between me and him, eager for him to win my approval. By the time Europe comes up in conversation, Bards is well and truly drunk.

'Look, no offence, but I'll be happy when this Wimbledon stuff is over,' he slurs, reaching over to Harley to punch him playfully on the arm. 'Then we can all hang out for the summer. The four of us.' He waggles his finger at me. 'Don't try to pretend like you two aren't a thing. I can tell something's going on here. Kat called it early, didn't you, babe.'

'Yeah, I knew,' Kat says, a little tipsy herself. 'We can go on double dates.'

I make a non-committal 'Mmm' sound.

'It's going to be fun,' Bards insists, unscrewing the lid of his whisky bottle, checking no one is looking and then taking a swig before offering it to Harley, who shakes his head. 'Go on, mate. No one is around and drinks here are expensive.'

'No, thanks,' Harley states.

Bards snorts, unimpressed. 'Suit yourself. Where was I? Oh yeah, a fun summer ahead now that Kat isn't going to leave us for some stupid other country and I'll have my boy Harley back with his tennis shit over.'

I frown at Kat. 'You're definitely not going to Europe?'

'I haven't made a decision yet,' she maintains, despite Bards's pointed sigh. Glancing at him, she adds quietly, 'But I think I'll probably cancel it. I can go to Europe another time. I like the idea of spending more time with you lot.'

'Exactly,' Bards says, reaching for her hand and lifting it to his lips. He kisses her knuckles and she gazes at him. It makes me feel sick.

Harley shifts in his seat.

'You've planned this trip for so long, Kat,' I point out, taking the opportunity to bring in a different point of view from the one she's heard a lot of recently. 'It's something you've *always* wanted to do. You don't have to make any rash decisions; you can see how you go.'

'I don't remember her asking for your opinion,' Bards says bitterly but with a bemused expression, as though he thinks it's funny for me to have an opinion at all.

'I'm not trying to sway you, Kat,' I drive on, ignoring him, 'and I'll support whatever decision you make. I just don't think you need to put pressure on yourself to decide now what you—'

'God, you really don't know when to shut up, do you?' Bards huffs.

'Hey, don't speak to her like that,' Harley snaps.

Bards glowers at him. Harley doesn't back down, his expression hard, his jaw tense. Then, Bards breaks into an unnerving grin, taking another swig from his whisky bottle. The barman has seen him and I watch with relief as he strides over to us. I don't warn Bards – I want him to be kicked out.

'You need to leave, sir,' the barman says firmly.

'Fine,' Bards says, looking at Harley with disdain. 'I know when I'm not wanted.'

CHAPTER TWENTY-SIX

Bards gets to his feet, stumbling and having to grip the back of a chair for balance. Without another word to any of us, he makes his way out of the bar back to the lobby.

'Bards, wait,' Harley says, heaving a sigh and leaping to his feet to go after him.

Shooting the barman a grateful smile, I push my chair back and get up as Kat does the same. She reaches over to grab my arm.

'I'm so sorry, Bills,' she says, her voice wavering. 'We never should have come. It was a stupid idea when tomorrow is such an important day for you and ... I'm so sorry. It's selfish. I just didn't want you to think I didn't care. We had a couple of drinks and I was going on about you ... Look, I wasn't thinking.'

'It's okay. This isn't your fault,' I assure her. 'High emotions and alcohol, that's all.'

'He shouldn't have spoken to you like that; I promise he's

not like this usually. He's kind, caring and sweet – when it comes to me, he's a bit …'

'Possessive?'

She sighs. I feel bad for being so blunt. I need to be careful. I don't want to push her away from me any further than she's already drifting.

'Kat, if you don't want to go to Europe because you don't want to break up with Bards, then I get it,' I add. 'You should do what *you* want to do, that's all.'

'Why does everything have to be so complicated?'

'I know, right?' I say, sharing a conspiratorial smile with her.

'Will you tell me what's going on with you and Harley?'

'Yeah, another time.'

Linking arms, we slowly stroll out the bar and through the lobby, stepping out into the cool evening air. We gingerly approach Harley and Bards, who are standing face to face on the pavement in the middle of a heated conversation.

'Uh oh,' I say in hushed voice, my stomach churning at the sight of them squared up to one another.

'This doesn't look good,' Kat whispers back, biting her lip.

Neither of them realize that we've caught up and we overhear the conclusion of whatever Harley is yelling at Bards.

'—and you know that. This is your last chance. Either you tell her or I will!'

'Tell me what?' Kat says sharply, dropping my arm.

Bards's eyes widen to saucers. Harley spins at her voice, flustered.

'You were talking about me, right?' Kat says to Harley. 'So, what is it that you need to tell me.' She looks at her boyfriend, who has gone pale. 'Bards?'

His jaw twitches. He glances at Harley, hissing, 'You fucking—'

'Tell me, Bards,' Kat orders fiercely as Harley refuses to cower under Bards's stare. 'Whatever it is, you need to tell me right *now*.'

Bards clears his throat, his expression softening as he gazes at her with appealing eyes. 'Look, it was nothing, babe. It was a mistake. I'd had a few drinks and this girl, she was all over me. I told her no, but she was persistent and I wasn't thinking, I was really drunk. It meant *nothing*.'

Kat physically recoils as he tries to reach out to her. She stares at him as I clasp a hand over my mouth.

'Did you sleep with her?' Kat croaks, her eyes glistening with tears. 'And don't fucking lie to me, because I'll find out the truth.'

He winces. 'Like I say, it meant nothing.'

Her face crumples. 'When? When was this?'

'Kat—'

'I asked you a question,' she yells, her voice echoing around the built-up street and causing passers-by to look over nosily at the commotion.

He looks shocked by her outburst. 'It was ... when you were at Wimbledon.'

She closes her eyes, a single tear falling down her cheek. 'I left my friend's match early to come back to you because you made me feel so guilty, and that whole time, you were with someone else? Is that right?'

'Kat, please, it only—'

'Don't talk to me ever again,' Kat says firmly, looking him right in the eye. 'I can't believe I almost cancelled Europe for you.' She glances at Harley. 'Thank you for trying to make him do the right thing.' Then, she leans in to kiss my cheek, whispering in my ear, 'I'll message when I get home.'

'Kat, wait,' I say, but she's already turned on her heel and marched to the road just as a taxi with its yellow light on approaches.

She must have seen it coming and decided it was the perfect time to exit. Can't say I blame her. She flags it, sliding into the back and shutting the door behind her. Bards rushes after her, but the car pulls away quickly on her instruction.

Watching the car disappear, Bards rounds on Harley, his expression and rolled-up fists making my nerves spike. I'm genuinely scared of what he might do, but Harley isn't fazed. He only takes a step towards him, blocking me.

'This is your fault. You're meant to be my friend,' Bards spits, leaning in inches from Harley's face. 'What the fuck is your problem?'

'I was being your friend by telling you to come clean,' Harley says calmly, refusing to flinch. 'You needed to tell her before she cancelled the trip of a lifetime for you.'

'You better never come near me again. You hear me?'

'Don't say things you'll regret, Bards. Take a deep breath, calm down and—'

'And what? You expect me to ever look you in the eye again? You're *pathetic*, Harley – you always have been. You were nothing before me and you'll be nothing without me. Just a piece of trash with no family and no friends. I took pity on you, mate. That's the only reason I stuck around. I felt sorry for you because I knew you were going nowhere.'

'Hey!' I cry, stepping out from around Harley.

'Oh here we go,' Bards says, sneering at me. 'Ice Queen coming to your defence.'

'Queen? Oh! A promotion! How unexpected!' I shoot back.

'Sorry, I should have said Ice *Bitch*.'

'I'm warning you,' Harley growls, moving closer to him, his eyes flashing with anger.

'You know I got you all wrong, Billie Dawson,' Bards continues, holding up his hands. 'I thought you were all prim and proper, a cold-hearted prude, but you must be a really good shag to make Harley completely turn his back on—'

Harley's fist moves so fast, it's a blur. He punches Bards square on the nose. Bards yelps in pain, his head jolting back as he stumbles from the force before he cups his face with his hands. Doubled over, he cries out, '*Fuck*, that hurt!' wiping the trickle of blood away from his lip with the back of his hand.

'Don't ever speak to her again – *ever*,' Harley says in a low, threatening tone that sends a shiver down my spine. 'Now go home, Bards.'

With that, Harley reaches for my hand and, taking it, drags me back into the hotel, across the lobby and towards the lift. Impressed, the receptionist gives him a thumbs-up as we pass. I glance back over my shoulder to see Bards still wincing in pain, rubbing his jaw with his hand before he shakes his head and starts to walk away.

'Are you okay?' I ask Harley quietly, still in shock as the lift doors ping open.

He gives a sharp nod, but his jaw is locked tight. We don't speak again until we get to my room. He comes in with me and the first thing I do is inspect his hand. His knuckles look sore. I march over to the hotel phone and call down for some ice to be sent up straight away. He slumps on the bed, burying his face in his hands. I don't know what to say, so I sit down next to him and put my arm around him. We sit there like that in silence until there's a knock on my door – it's the barman personally delivering the ice.

'I heard what happened,' he says to me as he hands it over, along with a tea towel. 'Please tell Mr Pierce thanks from us all. Whoever that guy was, he had it coming.'

I smile at him, retreating back into the room with the

small bucket of ice and grabbing a few lumps to wrap in the tea towel. Perching next to Harley, I gently pull his hand from his face and place the cold press against his knuckles. He lifts his head, sighing.

'I'm sorry,' he says, his forehead creased. 'I lost my cool.'

'Don't apologize! Thank you for protecting my honour,' I say, making him break into a small smile. 'Very noble of you. And *very* sexy.'

'Yeah?' He raises his eyebrows. 'That's something, then.'

'Are you okay?'

He nods slowly. 'Something like this was always going to happen. I don't know why I've stayed friends with him so long. He's bad news.'

'Because you're loyal. That's a good thing.'

'When he told me he'd cheated on Kat, he didn't even sound sorry,' Harley says, frowning as though he's still trying to get his head round it. 'He found it funny. He was ... almost proud of it. Like all of it was ... a game. I told him he had to tell her and he laughed. It tortured me all yesterday afternoon and today. I hated keeping this from you.'

'That's why you acted so strangely at dinner last night. Then when Kat was talking about cancelling her Europe trip ...'

'It wasn't fair for him to let her do that, especially when he didn't feel remorse for what had happened with that other girl.' He glances up at me. 'He'd do it again, and she'd have sacrificed a lot for him.'

'You did the right thing.'

'You're not mad at me for not telling you?'

'No, I understand why you didn't. He was your friend. You couldn't go behind his back when your loyalty lies with him – you had to try to get him to do the right thing first.'

His shoulders drop as he exhales. 'A tiny part of me really hoped he might.'

I kiss his cheek lightly and he turns his head to press his lips against mine, deepening the kiss and making my head go fuzzy to the point that I forget what I'm doing, letting the ice pack slip off his hand.

'Whoops, sorry,' I say, quickly pressing it against his knuckles again.

He wiggles his fingers. 'You think I'll be okay to play tomorrow?'

'Course. If anything, you'll play better,' I say, grinning at him. 'You've shown your menacing fighting spirit.'

'I might just about match yours.'

I bring my eyes up to meet his. 'Thanks again for tonight,' I say hoarsely, my heart rate quickening under his intense gaze. 'I really appreciate you looking out for Kat and for standing up for me. You were like . . . a sexy, sporty modern knight.'

He chuckles, leaning to rest his head on my shoulder before he says, so quietly I almost don't hear him, 'I'm not sure you were the one who needed rescuing, Dawson.'

CHAPTER TWENTY-SEVEN

Junior Championships, Wimbledon 2025
Mixed Doubles Quarter-Finals, Court 4
B. Dawson (GBR) & H. Pierce (GBR) vs
G. Jackson (USA) & C. Cox (USA)

Walking onto the court the next morning, I'm the most nervous I've been all tournament. Firstly, we're up against the American pair who beat us at the Roehampton finals, Jackson and Cox, both brilliant and tough opponents. Secondly, my dad and Tom are back in the stand to watch us today. And thirdly, the drama of last night has taken its toll. Neither Harley nor I slept well last night and our morale has taken a bit of a hit.

Kat messaged me last night to say Jess had met her at the station the other end and taken her home, and that she was sorry about everything that had happened with Bards. I was just glad she was okay. Harley hasn't heard from Bards and he doesn't expect to – as far as he's concerned, their friendship is over. He says that's a positive thing, but losing a friend – even one you've grown apart from; even one whose values don't match yours any more; even one as shitty as Bards – is sad when you've been through so much together.

As Harley unzips his bag to pull out his racket, I glance his way apprehensively.

He catches my eye and smiles. A warm, confident smile.

'We gave these two a bit of an easy ride at Roehampton – they'll be a lot more tired today, especially Jackson, who is still in the running in the girls' singles tournament. Let's beat them this time, yeah, Dawson?' he says quietly, winking at me.

'You know what? Let's,' I say determinedly.

He raises his eyebrows and laughs.

'What? Why are you laughing?'

'Because I know that look, the one on your face right now,' he says, grinning from ear to ear. 'It's like you were telling me, *As soon as you're on this grass, you can forget everything else and take back control.* These two don't stand a bloody chance.'

We win the first set four games to six, but it was a narrow victory, with both sides giving everything and hardly making any mistakes. In between sets, neither Harley nor I felt like we had it in the bag – we knew that Cox and Jackson were going to come back fighting, the two of them whispering hastily to each other as they strolled onto court for the second set, the strength of their resolve radiating from them as they fist-pumped.

But Harley and I aren't going to back down from a fight. Not today.

We keep our cool under pressure, learning from each other as we go along. He tries for every shot. I try to be a little more unpredictable.

It's working.

At three games to five in the second set, it's fifteen–forty in Jackson's service game. We're one match point away from winning the quarter-finals. I don't think Jackson and Cox can believe it. I watch from the net as Jackson selects a ball for her next serve, chewing on her lip. Her confidence is shaking. She's angry, but she's also scared.

Stepping up to the line, she bounces the ball before hitting a big, fast serve straight into Harley's body. He does all he can to get his racket behind it. The ball hits the frame and ricochets into the air out of court, nearly hitting the umpire on the way out.

He ducks, then announces, 'Thirty–forty'.

Still one match point away from the semi-finals.

'Keep the ball within the lines, yeah, Pierce,' I joke as I pass Harley on the way back to the baseline.

'Oh, is the umpire not a part of this?' he says innocently, before we share a smile.

I crouch, rising up on the balls of my feet, pulling my focus as Jackson prepares to serve. The ball flies towards me and is thankfully called, 'Out.' I exhale, moving forward a little, preparing to return again. That was really fast, and if it had been a few centimetres to the left, it would have been an ace for sure. Jackson is not giving up quite yet. Good.

She tosses up the ball and goes for her second serve. It zips over the net with topspin, dropping just in the service box and bouncing high. I power through the ball, returning it to Jackson, who remains on the baseline. She sends it back cross-court to me and I return it to her, trying to force an error.

Jackson spots Harley edging to the centre of the court looking to poach one of her cross-court shots and sends the ball back with amazing control straight down the tramlines past him. Harley watches it go over his right shoulder; nothing he can do. But I'm already running to cover him. Jackson has precision, but her speed and power can be lacking. Thankfully, that's the case now, and I'm able to get to the ball and play an effective, if clumsy, cross-court return, which travels in between Cox and Jackson. If I'd had more time to put more strength behind it, it could have been a winning point.

Jackson reaches the ball and attempts a lob over Harley, who has reacted to the last shot and swapped sides. The ball soars up, up over his head.

It drops down towards me from the sky.

My arm raised, I prepare to smash the ball and try to finish this rally and the match at the same time. Time seems to slow down. I can hear my shallow breathing. Out the corner of my eye, I see Jackson and Cox both retreating behind the baseline, preparing for my smash. They know that's how I play. It's always been one of my best shots. I'm the power; Harley's the flair. Every opponent we come up against has read that in our play. I know Jackson is probably furious at herself right now. I mean, she's given this to me. She knows how I will play this ball and she's doing all she can to get into position to try her best to return it.

It's the perfect time to take a risk. For once, I don't want to play it safe. I want to try something new, see if I can pull it off. I think about what Tom would do. And how Harley would play this ball. What would happen if I do something unexpected? I might lose the point, yeah. But I'm not so scared of that any more. There's always the next one.

Time to have a little fun.

I can't stop a smile as I drop my arm at the last minute and with a soft underarm slice, I send the ball skimming over the net, landing just a metre or so from it. The ball bounces low twice before anyone can even acknowledge what's happened.

The crowd on Court Four erupts.

Jackson's jaw drops. Cox has his hands on his hips. As

I turn around, I'm greeted by Harley, who pulls me into a giant hug, lifting me into the air, squeezing the breath out of me.

We're through to the semi-finals.

The next morning, I should be feeling on top of the world. I should be feeling excited, nervous, *ready*. Today, I am playing in the semi-finals of the Junior Championships of Wimbledon for the first ever mixed doubles tournament. I'm so close to achieving what I've wanted for such a long time. If we win today, we'll be playing in the final tomorrow.

But as I stand by the window in my hotel room, watching the grey clouds move in as the street below begins to wake up, I can't shake a deep feeling of unease.

When my phone rings and I see it's Dad calling, I know something is wrong.

I know before he's even said it.

'Billie,' he says in a raspy, panicked voice as I answer, 'it's Tom. He's collapsed and been rushed to hospital. They're taking him in for surgery now.'

There's a knock on my door.

Feeling numb, I open it, the phone pressed to my ear. Harley is on the other side dressed in his tennis gear and ready to head to the practice courts. He takes one look at my face and his falls, his eyes widening with fear.

'What is it?' he asks in a whisper. 'What's wrong?'

'Dad, I'm on my way,' I croak into the phone, tears spilling over.

We hang up and I fall into Harley's arms, already outstretched to catch me.

CHAPTER TWENTY-EIGHT

After seeing Harley and me win the quarter-finals, Tom felt elated and inspired. He woke early the next morning, sprang out of bed, ignoring the faint pain he was feeling to the left of his stomach, and got dressed in his T-shirt and shorts before grabbing his racket to head out.

Arriving on his own at the court, he decided to practise against the ball machine until someone else got there. He hit a few balls, moved to the net, and got distracted by a phone call. He forgot to move out the way as a tennis ball was launched from the machine, punching him right in the spot where that niggling pain was before. He yelped, but after the initial shock, he decided to carry on, despite the tenderness of his stomach.

A couple of people he knew from the club arrived at the court and invited him to join them for practice. By the time he left the court an hour or so later, he felt a little light-headed. On the way home, he began to feel dizzy. Too dizzy to walk. He stopped and leaned against a lamppost. A passer-by saw him and stopped to check he was all right. He said he was fine, but she didn't leave – she was a carer and could tell that something was wrong. She asked him what had happened and he told her. Then he collapsed. She called an ambulance. It turns out, he had ruptured his spleen. He was rushed straight to surgery with life-threatening bleeding.

The surgery has taken just over two hours so far.

The passer-by is a lady called Eleanor, who has had to leave but has asked me to message her with an update when Tom is out of surgery. Her kindness to a total stranger has been a spark of light in the dark horror of today.

Dad and I are sitting side by side on the hard chairs in the waiting area. Harley is on my other side, his arms folded across his chest. Nick is standing up, leaning against the wall. I was in such shock after Dad's phone call, I don't think I would have got here without both of them, neither of whom hesitated to get a taxi sorted right away, accompanying me on the long journey all the way here to the hospital.

Nick checks his watch and then takes a step towards me.

'Billie,' he says quietly, his head furrowed in concern, 'what would you like to do?'

I've been waiting for him to ask this question. I probably should have told him the decision I'd subconsciously made before I even got in the taxi. There's no choice here.

I shift to face Harley. 'I'm so sorry. I can't leave Tom.'

He smiles at me, reaching to take my hand in his. 'I know.'

Nick nods. 'I'll go and make the call.'

'And I'll go get some more coffees,' Harley offers. He leans in to kiss me on the cheek in front of Nick, in front of Dad. It's a statement; one I appreciate. One I need right now. He draws back, gazing at my watery eyes. 'You're making the right decision, Bills.'

'I know,' I whisper, my voice breaking.

Squeezing my hand before he lets it go, he gets to his feet. 'You want another coffee, Mr Dawson?'

'Matthew, please,' Dad insists, and Harley nods. 'Thank you, yes. Black, no sugar.'

Harley and Nick walk out together. Dad and I fall back into silence.

After a few minutes, Dad heaves a sigh and says, 'I'm sorry, Billie. I know how much you've been training, how much work you've had to do to get this far in the tournament. I'm sorry you have to pull out of the semi-finals today.'

'The tournament doesn't matter, Dad.' I smile weakly as a tear runs down my cheek. 'It's funny – suddenly, it doesn't feel important at all.' I pause, before quietly adding, 'I'm only sorry that I won't have another chance to make Mum proud.'

Dad looks at me, bewildered. 'What are you talking about?'

I bite my lip, debating whether to tell him the truth or not. I guess I can't give him a snippet and then not fully explain, but I feel a stab of guilt bringing Mum into this at all today when his brain is so clouded with worry about Tom.

Taking a deep breath, I start to explain. 'I lost the Fourteen and Under Girls' Final when she was watching. It turned out to be the last match she ever saw me play.'

Dad blinks at me. I was hoping that might be enough, but I read the confusion in his expression, so feel the need to be clearer.

'Mum died thinking that Tom was the winner and I was the loser.'

I hear Dad's sharp inhale of breath.

'It's okay, Dad,' I add hurriedly, desperate not to cause him more upset. 'I ... I've accepted that that's how it played out and I can't go back in time. But I thought that by winning at Wimbledon this time round, somehow I'd be honouring her memory. I wouldn't have completely let her down.'

'Oh, Billie,' Dad says, running a hand down his face before he swivels in his seat to face me. 'Is that what you've thought all these years?'

Talking about it out loud has inspired a fresh wave of tears and all I can do is nod as they stream down my cheeks, unable to push any words past the lump in my throat.

He shakes his head. 'That is not what your mum thought.'

'You're just saying that,' I say with a small sob, my face crumpling. 'But the truth is that I lost. I failed.'

'She didn't see it that way, not for a moment,' he says, frantically clasping my hands in his and forcing me to look up at him. 'Do you know what your mum got to experience that day at Wimbledon? Her fourteen-year-old daughter playing tennis at the most prestigious tournament in the world – and even more importantly, seeing you do what you do best. She never cared about the result! Truth be told, I honestly don't think your mum ever fully understood the points system in tennis. She never really knew who was winning or where we were in the match.'

A bubble of laughter escapes from my throat. Dad pulls a tissue out of his pocket and dabs at my cheeks. Suddenly, in this moment, I'm not a grown-up who can take care of herself. I'm a little girl who needs her dad to wipe away her tears.

'Your mum loved how you lit up when you played tennis,' Dad continues, his eyes gleaming as he smiles at me. 'She loved how you played with passion and focus and *heart*. She didn't care about the points or the rankings or any of that nonsense – she loved the game because *you* loved the game. All that mattered to her was that you were running about that court, so brilliant and happy and *alive* out there. Billie, you were never a loser. Not to me, not to Tom, and certainly not to your mother.'

'Really?' I whisper, my heart aching with her loss, but easing with his words, a weight that it's carried for years beginning to show signs of lifting.

'Really. I meant what I said to you the other day,' he says firmly. 'The only person who might have let anyone down in this family is me for letting you think for one moment that you were anything less than you are. Billie, you are such a talent.'

'Thanks, Dad,' I say gratefully through sniffles.

'I can tell you this: your mum would have been so proud of you today.'

'I didn't even play.'

'Exactly,' he says, nodding. 'You put your family and your love for your brother before anything else. You're here. That's what matters. That's something to be proud of.'

He draws me into a hug and I rest my head on his shoulder as he holds me tight. I cling to him, and when we finally break apart, he looks me in the eye and he tells me that everything is going to be okay.

I believe him.

Another long, torturous hour of waiting later, the doctor approaches us. Dad jumps to his feet. I follow hastily, and Nick and Harley stand right behind us, all four of us desperate and terrified of what she's about to say.

'He's going to be fine.'

I almost collapse with relief, my legs trembling unsteadily beneath me, but Harley is there, gripping my shoulders, holding me up so that when Dad turns to pull me into a hug, I'm there for him. Nick immediately starts asking the doctor sensible questions, listening intently to the answers so that Dad and I can have a moment to collect ourselves, safe in the knowledge that someone in our immediate circle knows exactly what's going on. When Dad lets me go, Harley's arm wraps round my waist. I'm not alone. I never have been.

Everything is going to be okay.

CHAPTER TWENTY-NINE

'I need to say something,' Tom announces from his hospital bed three days later.

I glance up from scrolling on my phone and Dad lowers his mug of coffee, having brought in his own flask from home. He could only cope with the first day of hospital coffee, and every morning after that, he's come in prepared.

Tom moves to push himself up more and both Dad and I spring into action, Dad rushing to support him while I plump the pillows behind him. Tom swats us both away, telling us he's *fine* and to stop fussing. He's not fine – recovery from surgery is going to take a while and he's going to be in hospital at least a few days more – but he does look a little better today. He's sleeping and eating well. His cheeks have more colour in them, the dark circles under his eyes are beginning to fade and his eyes are brighter. He seems more himself.

It's been a rough few days. His surgery went well, which was positive, but it was horrible to see him afterwards, so weak and medicated. I've been so worried about him, I've barely slept. When I walked in this morning and saw him sitting up and smiling at me, I almost crushed him with a hug and then I whacked him on the arm for being such a fucking idiot and playing sport when he'd been so ill. I know he's more himself because he whacked me right back and told me I wasn't allowed to yell at him when he's a patient.

'What is it, Tom?' Dad asks him attentively, taking a seat in the chair next to the bed, while I stand on the other side of him. 'What is it you need to say?'

Tom clears his throat. 'I'm not going to study law at York.' He pauses as Dad stares at him in bewilderment. 'I've been lying to myself. I think I've known for a while now that I don't want to be a lawyer. What I really want to do is work with animals.'

'*Animals*,' Dad repeats, aghast.

'Yeah, animals,' Tom confirms with a light laugh at Dad's expression. 'I don't know how, and I don't know in what capacity. I think I'd like to do veterinary medicine, so I'd have to redo some A-Levels – I don't think I can get on a vet course with English, history and politics. I was always pretty good at biology and chemistry.'

'Top of your class, if I remember right,' I chip in, and he gives me a grateful smile. 'I always did think it was a bit weird that you took those as AS-Levels and then dropped them.'

'I thought I wanted to focus on the subjects I needed for law school, which is what I thought I should do,' he admits. 'But after all this –' he gestures around him – 'I've realized ... well ... life's too short. You should do what makes you happy. Right, Dad?'

Dad inhales deeply. 'Absolutely.' He breaks into a wide smile. 'Tom, you should do whatever the hell you want. All I want is for you to be happy. Both of you.'

I can see Tom visibly relax, his whole body sinking into the bed with relief. When he turns to me, I'm smiling proudly at him, but he frowns.

'And now I need to tell you the truth, Billie.'

'Me?' I blink at him.

'Yeah. Okay, here goes. You can't be annoyed at me.'

'Don't be stupid! Of course I won't be.'

'All right.' He takes a deep breath. 'I never wanted to play doubles with you at Wimbledon.'

My jaw drops to the floor. '*Huh?*' is all I can manage.

He shrugs. 'I knew how much it meant to you and I didn't want to let you down. You were so determined and you worked so hard – I felt that I needed to be a part of it for you.'

'Did you want to play on the singles tour instead? Is that it?'

'No,' he says, finding the suggestion amusing. 'I didn't want to play full stop.'

I balk at his admission. 'Tom, you *love* tennis.'

'I do, but I don't love playing competitively. I don't care about rankings. That's why I've always been embarrassed about that Fourteen and Under win. Firstly, me winning that was pure luck – the other finalist had had food poisoning the day before – and secondly, the pressure of that win has been the *worst*.'

'The pressure?'

'Yeah, the pressure!' He tips his head back onto the pillow behind him, staring up at the ceiling. 'Everyone would refer to that win as though I was meant to go places, so I felt I had to keep playing competitively in some capacity or I'd be letting everyone down: you, Dad, Nick, Mum.' He sighs, closing his eyes. 'I resented winning so much because I felt trapped by the expectations of it.'

'I . . . I had no idea you felt like that,' I admit.

He offers a small smile. 'I was so relieved when we all agreed that pursuing tennis professionally was probably not going to happen. The doubles tour was so important to everyone, and I do love playing tennis, so I went along with it. But the truth is, I never really enjoyed the tournaments. I dreaded them.'

'God, I'm sorry, Tom,' I say, horrified. 'I never would have made you play if I'd known that you felt like this.'

'It's not your fault. It's mine,' he tells me firmly. 'Like I say, I've been lying to myself about a lot of things, but when something like this happens, you realize what's important.'

'Yeah, you do. Well, from now on, you never have to play doubles with me again.'

'That's not what I want,' he clarifies, giving me a pointed look. 'I love playing doubles with you. Tennis is part of who I am. But I don't want to take part in any tournaments any more. I want to find the fun in it again.'

'That, I actually understand,' I say through a smile. 'Recently I've been learning to find the fun in it, too.'

'Yeah, I can tell,' Tom says proudly. 'That drop shot in the quarter-finals was pretty inspired. I'd love to say it was me, but I think that may have been the influence of your new partner.' He sighs, a flicker of pain crossing his expression. 'I'm so sorry that you and Harley had to pull out of Wimbledon, Bills. It's all my fault. I cost you the win.'

'We've been over this – it was my decision.' I shoot him what I hope is a comforting smile. 'I really don't care, promise.'

He quirks a brow. 'Are you taking it well partly because you're so in *loooove*?'

My cheeks flare with heat. 'Tom!'

'It's true! You and Harley, the perfect match,' he teases.

'Shut *up*!' I hiss through gritted teeth, whacking his leg.

'You shut up!'

'Oh god, stop it, both of you,' Dad says, his voice raised.

I glare at Tom and he just looks back at me smugly. He's so annoying.

'Right, now *I* have an announcement,' Dad claims in his most authoritative voice. 'From now on, this family is going to be honest with each other. I think I speak on behalf of all three of us when I say that we're all proud of one another. Right?'

'Right,' Tom says.

'Sure,' I agree.

'Good, so if we have ... worries or issues or problems, then, you know –' he gesticulates awkwardly with his hands – 'we should ... you know ...'

Tom and I share a smile. It's so nice to see Dad like this, encouraging a more open household, but also kind of hilarious. It doesn't exactly come to him naturally.

'We should *talk* about them,' I say, helping Dad out.

'Exactly,' he says, pointing at me. 'We should talk about them.'

'Good idea, Dad,' Tom says.

'Great,' Dad says, leaning back in his chair with a satisfied expression.

'On that note, I have an issue I would like to discuss with the family,' Tom proffers.

'You have the floor,' Dad proclaims.

'Since it looks like I'll be at home a little while longer,' he begins, looking at Dad hopefully, 'any chance I can get a dog?'

I burst out laughing. Dad closes his eyes in despair. Tom grins at him excitedly. And something about the air in the room feels a lot lighter than it did before.

CHAPTER THIRTY

Two years later ...

Melrose's finest 🌿♥

> **Jess**
> The big day is here!
> Good luck, Bills!!
> How are you feeling?

> **Billie**
> Nervous
> Excited
> I think I might be sick

> **Kat**
> Nah, you've got this
> *Tu es incroyable!*

Jess
Jesus
She spends ONE term abroad and suddenly she's French

Billie
Do you remember when she got back from her Europe travels that summer after school and she'd basically convinced herself she was German?

Jess
Oh my god YES
She kept saying 'GUTEN MORGEN'
Every bloody day

Billie
Hahahahaha
Now it will be 'BONJOUR!' all the time

Kat
You know what?
I'm tempted to bin the glittery sign that I made for you specially, Billie

I have new friends in France you know
Ones that are NICE

Billie
Noooooo!
I need the glittery sign
Please still be my friend
Je suis désolé!

Kat
Fine, I'll bring the sign
And we can MAYBE still be friends

Billie
Merci!

Kat
You're lucky I'm so forgiving

Jess
Yes, that's it
I'm sure you staying friends with Billie has nothing to do with you hooking up with her hot brother at Christmas

Kat
JESS!!

Jess
In Rambler's of all places
Old school

Billie
Eugh
Please don't remind me
I try to block out that vision

Jess
There was so much tongue

Kat
JESS!!

Billie
!!!!!!!!

Jess
Mwahahahaha
I think it's cute
Are you excited to see him today, Kat?

Kat
No!
I mean yes!
As in, I'm not NOT excited
It will be nice!
Because I haven't seen him since . . . you know . . .
Then I was abroad and he was studying or whatever
But yeah, I don't care
It's not a big deal
He's great
It's cool
I'm cool
Whatever
Did he say anything about me coming today, Bills?

Jess
Wow

Billie
Oh my god

Jess
It's going to happen, isn't it

Billie
100%

Jess
Shotgun maid of honour

Billie
UM HELLO!
I'm his sister and her best friend!
Surely I'd be maid of honour

Kat
STOP IT, BOTH OF YOU
Can we embarrass Jess instead?
She's the one bringing an actual date today ...

Billie
That's true
I can't wait to meet Fran!
Tell her not to judge me if I lose

Jess
You're not going to lose
And Fran will think you're amazing no matter what the result

Her sports skills are zero, so she's already impressed

Kat
I still can't believe that you met through a university book club
It's so sweet and nerdy

Billie
Like a book itself
The perfect meet cute

Kat
Très adorable!

Billie
Oui! C'est magnifique!

Jess
Oh god
Please don't be this weird in front of her
She's a very cool person
I'd like her to still fancy me after this

Kat
Jess, she's a member of book club
How cool can she be?

Jess
VERY COOL THANK YOU

Billie
We promise not to embarrass you

Kat
I make no promises
You were mean about my French
Revenge shall be mine!!

Jess
Fine, I'm going to tell Tom that you said he was the best you'd ever had

Billie
OH COME ON

Kat
JESS!!
I'm never telling you anything
EVER AGAIN

Billie
On that note . . .
I'm going to go

> But thank you for distracting me from my nerves for a bit
> Even if it did involve gross chat about my twin

Jess
Always here for you, pal

Kat
You go win this BUCKS final
Wait, not bucks
I mean BACKS
Or is it BIKS?
No, that can't be it

> **Billie**
> Almost there
> It's the BUCS tennis championships

Kat
That's the one
Go SMASH it!
(get it?)

Jess
You make that same joke every time

Kat
Merde!

Billie
Hahahaha
I love you two

Jess
Right back atcha
Good luck!!
Can't wait to cheer you on

Kat
Look out for the glittery sign!

Jess
You won't be able to miss us xx

The British Universities and Colleges Sport Tennis Individual Championships Finals
B. Dawson (University of East London)
vs Z. Clarke (Loughborough)

I'm leading 6–4, 5–2.

Clarke is serving. It's fifteen–forty. Match point.

Match point. Oh my god, I could win.

She has a fast serve and she'll be serving to my forehand because she knows it's weaker than my backhand. Exhaling steadily, I stare across the court at her as I crouch into position. She tosses the ball and swings her arm up and over it, but she knows as well as I do that it's going into the net. It was a poor toss – she should have left it. The ball hits the top of the net with a loud smack that echoes around the court. She went big with power, big enough to make a shiver roll down my spine.

Gasps ripple around the spectators. I gulp.

'Second serve, Clarke,' the umpire says.

Hold your nerve, Dawson, I tell myself.

When I decided I'd have a go at playing singles matches again on joining the team at UEL, I never thought I'd be good enough to make it this far. I thought I needed someone else on the court with me to rely on, but I was wrong. I've played better than ever this tournament.

One point. Just one point. I don't want to bottle this. Please don't let me bottle this.

Out the corner of my eye, I can glimpse the glitter of Kat's sign glinting in the lights. She's been cheering the loudest – as usual – all match. She's next to Jess, who's leaning into Fran to whisper something in her ear. On Fran's other side is Tom, Dad and Nick, none of whom have missed a match this whole tournament. They've been there to cheer me on for every single game.

And next to his uncle is the person responsible for me being here in the first place. The person who encouraged me to try out for the singles events. The man who believed I could win when I'd convinced myself I couldn't. The man I couldn't be without. Ever.

Harley Pierce.

It's funny – for so long I regretted losing that final at Wimbledon when I was fourteen, but now that I'm here, I wouldn't change a thing. Not one point of one game of one match. Every loss and every win was leading me right here to this moment.

And it all led me to him.

While Clarke takes her time to select the next ball for her second serve, I glance over to Harley. He catches my eye and smiles. My heart soars, as it always does when he looks at me that way. I shoot him a grin and he nods, suppressing a laugh. He's seen me smile like this before and he knows what it means.

It means I've made up my mind. This next point is mine.

Acknowledgements

A special thank you first and foremost to my wonderful editor Tierney Holm. It has been such an honour to work with you on this project. I have had so much fun writing this book and a lot of that is down to your brilliant guidance and endless sparkling enthusiasm. Huge thanks to you, the fabulous Yasmin Morrissey, and the Simon & Schuster editorial team for giving me this opportunity. Thank you to the design team for a stunning cover and to the marketing, publicity and rights teams who work so hard to get the book out into the world. I've loved every minute working on this with you all and I hope you're as proud of it as I am.

Thank you to my amazing agents, Lauren, Callen and Paul, and everyone at the Bell Lomax Moreton agency. Without your organisation and encouragement, I'd be completely lost – thank you for always cheering me on.

Special thanks to Nick Searle-Donoso and the International Tennis Federation for answering my questions and for all your help with my research into ITF Junior Tennis. Although all the characters and a Mixed Doubles event at Junior Wimbledon are fiction, this book was created from a love of tennis and greatly influenced by the ITF Junior tournaments that are played all over the world, so thank you for inspiring, developing and supporting the young, talented tennis players who go on to inspire all of us.

Huge thanks to Alice, my wonderful friend and a brilliant doctor who took the time to advise on the medical elements of the book. I'm so lucky to have you.

To all my family and friends, thank you, as ever, for your continued support as I muddle my way through the haze of deadlines, but mostly for always making me laugh (including at myself), something I've discovered to be one of the most important components of good writing and life in general. You're the best.

And finally, a great big thank you to the readers of *Game, Set, Matched*. I wrote this story in the hope that, if you're already a fan of tennis, it will capture your heart, and if you're new to the sport, it will win you over. Either way, this is really a story about two people who find themselves when they find each other and who fall in love along the way – the very best kind, in my opinion. Thank you for choosing it.

Also by Ivy Bailey

Durham University have the best women's football team in the League, and their star striker, Sadie McGrath, hopes to be scouted. The men's team is . . . less impressive and facing relegation.

But now Sadie has been asked to train the new striker, Arlo Hudson, who has just moved over from the US. The other girls think he's dreamy, but Sadie can't stand him.

What will happen when the two spend so much time together . . . Will Sadie be out of his league?